To

MW01225734

A BRIEF MOMENT IN TIME

Thank you for always
being my friends

William R. Dickson

A BRIEF MOMENT IN TIME

Short Stories

William Wayne Dicksion

iUniverse, Inc.
New York Lincoln Shanghai

A BRIEF MOMENT IN TIME
Short Stories

iUniverse books may be ordered through booksellers or by contacting:

iUniverse
2021 Pine Lake Road, Suite 100
Lincoln, NE 68512
www.iuniverse.com
1-800-Authors (1-800-288-4677)

ISBN: 0-595-34594-8

Printed in the United States of America

Contents

The Black Bear

It was an early summer morning. The little white gulf clouds were drifting lazily across the blue sky. The birds were singing. The bees were buzzing. Every flying, creeping or crawling thing was busy doing whatever it was supposed to be doing. I was almost five years old, and I, too, was busy being part of that glorious morning.

In the pasture nearby, I heard a calf bawling for its mother. I guessed it had gotten lost and was either frightened or hungry. I heard the mother moo a reply. I knew that all was well with the calf. The mother cow would take care of the problem.

I heard my mother calling me. I ran to the house to see what she wanted, or what I had done wrong. She wanted me to go to the neighbor's house, down the road about a mile or so, to borrow a cup of sugar. Mother wanted to bake some cookies. The baking of cookies seemed like a great idea to me, and I really didn't mind going after the sugar. I could be back in no time. Mother gave me a small Mason fruit jar with a lid on it so I would not spill the sugar, and I was off down the road in a jiffy. The road was little more than a two-rutted path that marked the place where horses pulled wagons across the land. A few people had cars, but most farmers still used horse-drawn wagons for transportation. My father's land was on the left side of the road, and our neighbor's land was on the right. The neighbor's land was fenced because it was pastureland, and he usually had cows grazing there. Sometimes there was a bull with the cows. We were not supposed to go through the fence, because the bull would chase you. I didn't know what he would do to me if he caught me, and I sure didn't want to find out.

The sand in the ruts of the road was soft and warm. It felt good to my bare feet. I saw a grasshopper with its tail sticking in the sand. My older brothers had told me that grasshoppers lay their eggs in the warm sand so that the warm sand will hatch the eggs. I wanted to stay and watch the eggs hatch. I watched for a while and nothing happened. The grasshopper just sat there with its tail sticking into the sand. I knew I couldn't wait all day; my mother expected me back with that cup of sugar.

I started on down the road. Up ahead a few hundred feet, I saw something sitting beside the road. It was big and black. I couldn't figure it out, so I hid behind a little hackberry bush which was growing beside the road, to take a good look at this thing. It wasn't a cow. It wasn't a horse. It wasn't any kind of farm animal I had ever seen. The longer I looked at it, the more it looked like a big, black bear! Now, that was not something I had planned on having to deal with on this trip to get the sugar.

This thing was between me and where I had to go. I couldn't turn around and go back. There was no way that I was going to convince my mother that there was a bear on the road. If I went back, I would get a scolding, at best. Another thing, I wanted them cookies. I decided to climb through the fence and go way around the bear. I thought the bull might be in that pasture. I didn't see him, but that didn't mean he wasn't there. There were a lot of places where a bull could be hiding. I figured that even if he saw me, he might be busy grazing and maybe he would leave me alone. If he did chase me, I could run pretty fast, and I could crawl back through the fence, or I could climb a blackjack tree. A blackjack tree is a kind of scrub oak. Blackjack trees do not grow very big, but they are big enough for me to climb to get away from an angry bull! I didn't know what I would do if that bull got me up a tree. How would I get down? Climbing through a barbed wire fence was no easy matter either, and I sure didn't want to get my britches caught on the barbed wire with that angry bull after me. Well, I would just have to deal with that problem when and if it happened.

I ran from blackjack tree to blackjack tree, finding my way through the neighbor's pasture, getting around that ol' bear until I felt I had traveled far enough that I would be past the bear. When I got back to the road, I looked back and I couldn't see the bear. I figured if I couldn't see him, he couldn't see me.

I ran on to the neighbor's house. She was there, all right, and filled my jar with sugar. She even gave me a glass of buttermilk. I hoped she would have some cookies, since she had plenty of sugar, but she didn't offer me any. I guessed she didn't have any, and if you are not offered, you are sure not supposed to ask. If you ask for cookies, and they don't have any, they would be embarrassed. It just ain't nice to ask.

I started home with the sugar, and then I remembered I had to go around that danged ol' bear again! I knew I was taking too long getting home with the sugar, but I just didn't dare go down the road and face that bear. I had to go all the way around again, so I ran all the way home.

Mother wanted to know why I had taken so long. I didn't dare tell her about the bear, so I told her about watching the grasshopper laying its eggs and waiting to see them hatch. She looked at me kinda funny, but she didn't say much—she just scolded me for inventing such a story. In those days, I was suspected of stretching a story from time to time, but I was telling the truth this time. At least part of it was true.

That afternoon, Mother and Dad had to go into town to get some supplies. I guess Mother needed to buy some sugar. So Dad told me to go out in the pasture and bring in Ol' Sam and Ol' George. Ol' Sam and Ol' George were our team of mules. They were not old; we just called them that. We had horses, but Dad liked the mules better for pulling the wagon. He said the mules could walk faster.

It didn't take me too long to find the mules. They were resting in the shade of a big ol' cottonwood tree. They saw me coming, and right away they knew that Dad had work for them to do. They wanted no part of it, so they started to run. I was up to their tricks, and I could run pretty fast, so I headed em' off and got them started for the barn. It took me a while, but I got them into the corral. Then I had to shut the gate. The gate was made of four strands of barbed wire with a gatepost at the end. The gatepost was heavy and I had to drag it to get it into place where I could get the wire loop around the bottom of the post. The wire loop would hold the post in position until I could get the wire hooked around the top of the post to shut the gate.

The loop at the top was too high. I couldn't reach it. I thought about laying the gate down and going to tell Dad that I couldn't close the gate. I knew that if I laid the gate down to go to the house, those danged mules would run off again, and I knew that failure was just not an option with my dad. So I reconsidered and decided that I had better figure some way to close that gate.

There was a short length of rope lying nearby, so I tied the rope to the end of the gatepost, climbed the fence, and got the post in the wire loop at the top. I snagged a little hole in my britches getting down from the fence, but I had won a victory over that gate, and I was feeling pretty proud about that. Anyway, Mother probably wouldn't even notice the tear in my clothes.

I went back to the house to tell Dad that the mules were in the lot. When I walked through the door, Mother asked, "What happened to your britches?"

Having to explain to her about climbing the fence to close the gate took some of the pleasure out of my victory over the gate. Dad looked kinda pleased, but he would never tell me that he was pleased; he was just not made that way. I had only done what I was supposed to do, so I had not earned any praise.

I went with Dad back to the barn. I wanted to watch him harness the mules. Dad was very good with animals. He liked animals, and they liked him. Even Ol' Sam, who was a very contrary mule, had a real respect for Dad. It might have been because Ol' Sam knew that Dad tolerated no nonsense from man or beast. The harness was heavy, and it took a pretty strong person to throw it up onto the backs of the mules and strap it into place. The first thing he had to do was put on the bridle; then he put on the collar. The collar is a very heavily padded device that fits around a horse or a mule's neck and rests against the animal's shoulders. After he got the mules harnessed, he backed them up to the wagon and hooked them to it. They were hooked to the wagon with chains called trace chains. The animals were controlled with long, leather straps called lines. Dad had the lines in his hands and we climbed upon the wagon, and drove it around to the front of the house for Mother to get in.

My older sister and two older brothers had been hoeing weeds in the cornfield all morning, but they were going to town with us this afternoon. We normally did not go to town in the afternoon. It took too long to get to town, but I guess they figured that we could get back before dark. It was summertime and the sun didn't go down until later in the evening. My sister was the oldest of us kids. She was ten. She was almost an adult. She could ride on the seat with Mother and Dad, but my brothers and I had to ride in the bed of the wagon. I liked to stand and hold onto the seat of the wagon. My chin would just rest on the back bracing of the seat, and I could look out between Mother and Dad sitting in the front. They would have their feet resting on the dashboard. It was called a dashboard because its purpose was to keep the dirt, which was kicked up by the mules, from hitting you in the face or landing in your lap.

We were going down the same road I had taken to go get the cup of sugar, and I was wondering if that bear might still be sitting beside the road. I didn't know how long a bear would stay in the same place, but he might still be there. I was watching the mules as they walked. Their heads would go up and down as they moved, and their ears would go back and forth as they walked. If something was wrong, the mules would usually be the first to notice it. Their heads would come up, and they would start looking all around to see what might be unusual. Their ears were very sensitive, and they could rotate them all around to pick up even the slightest sound. I knew that Ol' Sam would be the first to notice if the bear was still there, but he wasn't showing the slightest indication that he sensed anything wrong. His head was going up and down, up and down, in rhythm with his walking, and his ears were just going back and forth, steady as you please.

Pretty soon, way up ahead, I could see the black bear still sitting right in the same place beside the road. I was very pleased because now I could explain to Mother why I had taken so long to get the sugar. I wasn't worried about the bear this time. I knew that those mules would notice that bear long before we got to it, and for sure Dad could handle any ol' bear.

I watched the mules to see when they would notice the bear, but nothing was happening. Their heads were just going up and down, and their ears were just going back and forth, back and forth. I wondered if the mules were asleep and just not paying attention. But I was pretty sure it didn't work that way with mules. Ol' George was a calm and steady animal, and he would trust Dad's judgment in most matters. But Ol' Sam wouldn't trust anything except his own instincts, so I watched him the closest. Nothing was happening. We were getting closer and closer, and no one was seeing the bear but me. I thought maybe I should tell Dad about the bear, then I thought, *No, that don't seem like a good idea.* I wondered, *Why is that bear sitting so still?* I didn't know much about bears, but I was pretty sure that a bear wouldn't be just sitting there with a whole wagon load of people coming down the road towards him. The closer we got to that bear, the less it looked like a bear. And we were getting pretty close.

My mother and sister were just sitting in the seat beside Dad. They didn't see anything. My two brothers were sitting with their feet hanging over the tailgate of the wagon, arguing about something, so naturally they wouldn't see anything. The thing that made me begin to wonder if it really was a bear was the mules; their heads were just going up and down, with their ears going back and forth, just as calm as you please. Now the wagon was going by this thing, and I could see it real clear. It was not a bear at all. It was nothing but a burned-out, old stump! It really made me mad that I had gone to all that trouble to go so far around an old, burned-out stump!

Boy! Was I glad I had not told Mother about that bear. My reputation for being a little loose with the facts would not have improved one bit with that story. So the best thing for me to do was just lie down in the bed of the wagon and take a nap.

A Brief Moment in Time
William Wayne Dicksion

The Flying Rabbit

One of our milk cows was due to give birth. When she did not show up one morning with the rest of the cows, Father figured she had given birth during the night. He told me and my older brother, J.D., to go find her. He wanted us to check if the cow was all right and to determine if the calf had been born. The pasture area was rather large, with many small hills and ravines that had lots of trees and bushes. There were plenty of places for a cow to hide to give birth.

It was about 10 o'clock, on an early summer morning. J.D. was seven and I was five; plenty old to take on the serious responsibility we had been given. We knew that only our best effort would be accepted as good work. We had no choice but to find the cow and her calf, or at least find out if she had given birth to the calf. It was a beautiful day and we knew this was going to be an adventure. We were barefoot, and the best place to walk was along the well-beaten cow trails which laced the pasture area. The trails were about a foot wide, and the cows always followed the easy terrain to wherever they wanted to go, which was always to food, water or shelter. The grass and weeds along the trails were about a foot high, so the trails were not hard to follow. There were sweet-smelling flowers along the way, with birds, rabbits, ground squirrels, horned toads, lizards, and an occasional snake for us to see. There were many dry land turtles we called terrapins. We weren't looking for any of these. We were looking for Ol' Brownie and her calf.

Ol' Brownie is the name we had given the cow we were looking for. She was not old—that was just the name we had given her. Most of the animals' names were preceded by the term ol', like Ol' Baldy, Ol' Red, Ol' Roan, etc. Ol' Brownie was only four years old, which was young for a milk cow. This was her second calf. So she already knew how to have a baby. We were not worried about her, but we still had to find her and make sure that she and her calf were all right.

After searching the hills and several ravines, we came upon the cow and her calf. Ol' Brownie had given birth by the creek, under a big elm tree where there was shade and fresh water. There was only a little grass and weeds under the tree, so the baby would not have too much trouble getting up to be nursed by its mother. The calf was lying on the ground, and the mother was cleaning it by licking its hair with her tongue. Every place the mother cow would lick the calf, the calf's hair would be pretty and wavy. I was thinking that the women were always trying to get their hair to be wavy. All they had to do was to let that cow lick their hair and it would be wavy.

The calf was beautiful. It was all black except its legs and face; they were snow white. Its nose and eyes were black and shiny. We could tell the mother was really proud of her calf, and she had every right to be proud; it sure was a nice calf. It was a little heifer, so we would keep it, and one day it would be a milk cow. When the calf stood up, it looked like it was wearing white stockings. We decided to name it White Socks. She would be called Ol' White Socks.

It had not gotten up to feed yet, so we had to wait and make sure the calf got up to suckle the milk from its mother. Once a calf gets up and feeds, it is going to be all right. While we were waiting for the calf to nurse, we gathered some wild plums from a plum thicket nearby. The plums were bright red when they were ripe. These were nice and sweet so we ate all we could. We would have gathered some to take home, but we didn't have a container to put them in. The calf soon got up on very wobbly legs, and found its mother's milk and we knew it was going to be OK.

It was about 12 o'clock, and time for dinner. We called the midday meal dinner. The evening meal we called supper. The midday meal was the big meal of the day. Supper was a light meal of milk and bread. It was not considered good to eat a large meal before going to sleep. It could cause you to have a nightmare.

On the way home, we saw a young rabbit and decided to catch it for dinner. A young rabbit would make a very good meal. We chased and chased the rabbit. It ran this way and that way in the tall grass and weeds. Each time when we were just about to catch it, it would jump sideways, and we would miss our grab. The rabbit was getting tired, and we were getting tired, too. We were sure we were just about to catch it, when it ran into a hole in the ground. That was not too bad because we knew how to get the rabbit out of a hole. We cut a stick from a green willow tree with our pocketknives. We always carried pocket knives. The stick was about three feet long, with a fork at the small end. We pushed the forked stick into the hole, pressed it against the rabbit's fur, twisted the stick, and tried to pull the rabbit out. We could feel the rabbit, but we could not get a grip on its fur. We pulled the stick out to see if the fork on the stick might be broken, thinking that might be why we couldn't get a grip on the rabbit.

When we pulled the stick out, the rabbit was following the stick. It was gray and white like a rabbit. We could see its eyes and ears, so all we had to do was grab it when it came out of the hole. But when it came out, it did not run as we expected, but instead, it flew away! J.D. and I stood there and watched the rabbit fly away. We were dumbfounded. We knew that a rabbit could not fly, but we had both watched this one fly right off into the sky.

J.D. said, "I don't think we better tell anyone about this."

I asked him, "Why not?"

J. D. said, "No one is going to believe us."

"We both saw it happen. They've got to believe us."

He shook his head and said, "I still don't think we ought to tell them."

We walked home in silence, both thinking about what we had just seen.

When we got home, Mother had dinner on the table, and everybody was eating. We sat in our regular places and made our report to Dad about Ol' Brownie and her calf. While we were eating our dinner of fried chicken, biscuits, flour gravy, and beans, I told the story of the flying rabbit. By the time I finished telling the story, everybody was laughing so hard that they couldn't eat their dinner.

J.D. just looked at me and said, "I told you not to tell them."

Later, while thinking about what happened, I realized that there was a horned owl in the hole that the rabbit ran into. While we were poking into the hole, it was an owl we were feeling with the stick. The stick would not get caught in the owl's feathers, so we could not pull it out. When we did pull the stick out, the owl had enough of being poked with a stick and decided to come out and fly away. When the owl was coming out of the hole, we thought it was the rabbit we had chased into the hole. The owl was the same color as the rabbit. It had big round eyes like a rabbit. The horned feathers on its head looked like a rabbit's ears. We were sure it was a rabbit. When it flew away, we were sure we had seen a rabbit fly.

To a couple of little boys, it was an honest mistake.

A brief moment in time
William Wayne Dicksion

The Dragon

It was a late autumn day in 1930. My two older brothers and I were working with a pile of logs. We were cutting wood to be used for cooking, and we were also laying up a supply of wood we would need for heating the house in the winter. J.D. and I were sawing the logs into block lengths, and my oldest brother, Everett, was splitting the blocks to make them easier to store, and to make the wood better for burning.

One of our neighbors was visiting our farm, and he was talking to our father. While they were walking about the farmyard, our father stopped by to see how my brothers and I were doing with our chore of cutting wood. The two men sat on blocks of wood talking while we worked.

We were talking about being anxious for Dec. 2nd to come, which was the beginning of fur-hunting season, so we could go into the large forested area between our farms and catch animals for their fur. It was our custom to trap the animals and skin them, and prepare their hides to be sold so we would have money to spend at Christmas time. We were poor and selling the pelts of the animals was the only way we could get money to spend for other than the necessities of living. It was a very important event for us, and we were looking forward to it.

The neighbor was listening to our conversation and joined in to tell us that we should be careful because there was a dragon which lived in the woods where we were proposing to hunt.

We were country boys and we knew about every kind of animal that lived in those woods, but we had never seen a dragon. We reasoned that since our neighbor was a full-grown man, perhaps he knew something that we did not. Taking that into consideration, we were all listening intently to what he was telling us. The look on our father's face gave me cause to think that perhaps our neighbor was just trying to scare us. I was not sure, and Dad was not denying the story, so I decided that perhaps I should listen with concern.

The neighbor told us that the dragon had wings and could fly if it needed to, to catch us. There were hawks and owls and a few eagles that lived in the forest, so perhaps there might be a dragon, also.

I asked the neighbor, "What do dragons eat?"

He replied, "Their favorite food is children, but they will eat a pig or a chicken if they can't catch any children."

That bit of information made me and my brothers pay a lot closer attention to the story he was telling.

He said, "I saw one just a couple of weeks ago in the north edge of the woods."

On our normal hunting trips, we seldom went all the way through the woods to the north side. The story he was telling us gave me reason to think that maybe we should not go to the north side of the big woods.

Dad and the neighbor got up from their seats on the blocks of wood and walked to the barn. They were both kind of grinning when they walked away. It seemed strange to me, but I really didn't know what to make of the story about the dragon.

Everett said, "Ah, don't pay any attention to him; he is just kidding."

We continued cutting the wood. Over the next two months, we forgot all about the story.

December came; the weather was cold, so the fur would be good to sell. The weather needs to be cold for a few days before the fur will take a good grip on the skin. If you take the animal before the weather gets cold, the fur will not hold; it will just drop of the skin and the fur is no good. We found some time that we did not have to be busy doing work around the farm, so we took our 22-caliber rifle and went into the woods to see if we could catch a opossum, a skunk, a civet cat, or we might get lucky and catch a muskrat. The price of the pelts was a deciding factor in determining what we would hunt for. The pelt of an opossum was worth about two dollars. The skin of a skunk was worth about four dollars, and a muskrat was worth about nine dollars. I don't remember ever catching a muskrat, but we looked for one anyway.

We would remove the skins and stretch them over a board, scrape the excess tissue from the hide, and hang them up to cure. No one would pay for a raw skin. The skins had to be cured and dried, ready to be shipped to the people who used them for making coats and capes. Skinning and preparing the pelt of a skunk was a smelly job, but the hide was worth a lot of money, so we did it.

We were not having much luck catching animals. We had been out almost all day, and all we had to show for our time were two small opossums. When we had just about decided to call it a day and go home, we came upon the tracks of a skunk. We could tell by the tracks that he was a big one. Maybe worth five dollars. We began following the tracks. The tracks kept leading us deeper and deeper into the woods. The forest was very dense. The fall rain had left the leaves wet and we made very little noise as we walked. There could be anything hiding in all that brush and it could creep right upon you before you would be aware of its presence.

After about an hour of tracking, we felt we were getting close to the animal we were hunting. We could tell by the tracks that the skunk was only a short distance ahead of us. We were moving faster and faster trying to close the gap, when all of a sudden we found ourselves on the north side of the big woods. The tracks we were following led on across a meadow.

Beyond the meadow, there was a creek with a stand of trees along both sides. We felt sure the animal we were hunting would take shelter among those trees. We were continuing on across the meadow when, on a grassy slope beyond the creek, we saw an apparition coming down the hill to the creek with its black wings flapping.

What should we do? Our quarry was just ahead among those trees by the creek. The dragon would reach the creek before we could. At best, we were going to lose the value of the pelt we were seeking. If the dragon was as bad as the neighbor had said it was, then we might lose a lot more than that pelt. It soon became obvious that the dragon had seen us and was coming in our direction. There were frightful sound coming from that beast and it was without a doubt coming after us. Both J.D. and I were shouting for Everett to shoot it! Everett drew a bead and fired. The dragon folded its wings and began running back up the hill. It quickly disappeared into the trees at the top of the hill.

We gave up on our chase of the skunk and walked home carrying the two opossums. When we got home, we told Dad about the dragon.

"You didn't shoot at it, did you?" He exclaimed.

"Yes, we shot at it and it ran back up the hill."

"Did it seem to be hurt when it was running up the hill?"

"No, it was running pretty good and it didn't seem to be hurt."

Dad heaved a big sigh of relief and said, "That is good news. How did you happen to miss? You can shoot better than that."

Everett replied, "I don't think I missed, but I must have because it sure was running! It looked just like a man when it was running."

At that time, the neighbor rode up in his horse-drawn wagon into the farmyard and showed Dad the hole in his coattail.

"How could you have gotten a hole like that in your coat-tail and not have a wound on your body?" Dad asked.

Then he showed Dad how he had pulled his coattail up over his head and was waving it to frighten us as he came down the hill.

Dad said, "You are damn lucky you didn't get shot. Those boys shoot a rifle pretty good."

The neighbor agreed he was lucky and he said, "I will never pull a damn crazy stunt like that again." He gave a nervous laugh as he drove away in his wagon.

A brief moment in time
William Wayne Dicksion

The Christmas of the Little Red Wagon

It was 1932 and our nation was in the grips of the Great Depression. The central region of the United States was experiencing a severe drought, and the people were having a difficult time.

I was seven years old, the fourth in a family of five children. We had worked all year to grow and harvest fields of cotton, corn, and wheat. The crops had been good, but because of the depression, we were unable to sell what we had grown. This was the second year we had not made enough money to pay even the expenses of the year before. The debt was piling up. The only payday a farmer gets is when he sells what he has produced. The drought and the depression occurring at the same time made it necessary for Father to mortgage the farm to get money to plant new crops.

We were so poor that our father had to wrap his feet in burlap when he worked in the fields to save his shoes for when he went into town. The only things we could sell were butter and eggs. The money received from the sale of this produce was used to buy necessities such as salt, baking powder, vanilla, and medicines.

My two older brothers, my sister, and I rode a bus to the school, located several miles away in a small farming town. Everyone in the town was poor, even the merchants. They depended on the farmers to buy their merchandise. When the merchants had to close their stores, it created a hardship for everyone. The people had to travel a greater distance to get supplies. The economy was so bad that many were going hungry, some were starving.

We had food because we had animals. We had cows for milk and butter, chickens for meat and eggs, pigs for meat and oil. We had fresh fruit and vegetables from our orchard and garden. We preserved food by canning in the summer, and we used what we had canned to get us through the winter. We gathered pecans and black walnuts that grew wild along the creek. The people who lived in the little towns did not have these advantages. Our cows produced more milk than we could use. We gave some to the people who came at milking time. They were proud, embarrassed to accept charity, but they had no choice. For some, it was the only food they would have. They did not always express their gratitude with words, but their faces said it plainly.

We were poor, but we were blessed in many ways. I look back on these times with fond memories.

Each year at Christmas time, the school put on a play. I was one of the Three Wise Men. We practiced singing, "We Three Kings of Orient Are," until I could sing it in my sleep. In fact, from time to time, I still wake up humming the song. It left an indelible mark on my memory.

The Christmas tree stood on the stage at the end of the gymnasium. It was decorated with handmade ornaments and chains made of colored paper cut into strips, the ends pasted together to form links. We also hung strings of popcorn. Mistletoe grew wild along the creeks; we gathered and placed it on the bare branches to add greenery.

After the play, gifts from under the tree were passed to the students. There was a gift for each student. The gift was a red-mesh bag that contained an apple, an orange, nuts, and a few pieces of hard candy. That was the only Christmas gift most of the children would receive. I looked forward to receiving the gift. It was the only time I would get an orange–I would not see another for a year.

Money for buying these gifts was obtained by holding a box supper in the autumn after harvest time. The women prepared boxes of food and wrapped them in gaily-colored paper decorated with ribbons; some baked a pie or a cake. The people would gather at the gymnasium, and the boxes of food would be auctioned.

The young men competed in bidding for the boxes that had been prepared by the prettiest girls. These boxes, even in those hard times, would bring the enormous price of two or three dollars. It was quite a compliment to the girl when the food she had prepared sold at the highest price. It was the talk of the town for days.

Christmas Eve of 1932 was a crisp, cold winter night. The bus did not run at night. We children walked to the school to attend the Christmas event. Our mother and father never attended these events. I think they felt their clothes were inappropriate. I would have been proud to have them witness my performance in the play.

After the pageant, we walked home. While walking home on the dirt road, our feet made crunching sounds as we stepped on the frozen clods. A few stars illuminated the light covering of snow. We tried to keep our hands warm by stuffing them in our pockets. We talked about the Christmas play and the people we saw. Because it was so cold, our breath turned to steam. We had fun watching the steam coming out of our mouths as we talked, making it look like we were smoking.

By the time we got home, we were tired and cold. Mother, Father, and our baby brother had already gone to bed, but there was a fire in the wood-burning stove. I wanted to eat my apple before I went to bed. I opened the bag to get the apple–it fell on the floor and rolled under the bed. I crawled under the bed to get it. Lo and behold, there was a little red wagon! It was gleaming red, with yellow wheels and black tires. The tongue and frame were black, and the wheels had silver hubcaps. It was beautiful. I couldn't believe my eyes.

Where could it have come from? Mother and Dad had no money for buying something like that! They had tried to conceal it so they could surprise us in the morning. I could not hide my excitement. When I crawled out from under the bed, my sister and brothers saw the expression on my face and looked under the bed to see what had caused it. They, too, were astonished at what they saw. We realized that somehow they had managed to buy one gift that we could all share. I was so excited I could hardly sleep. I lay in my bed thinking of the sacrifice our parents had made to buy such an expensive present.

The next morning, we all pretended to be surprised when our father gave us the gift. I later learned that they had gotten the money for the gift by selling a calf.

We rode the wagon on the paths and trails made by animals. There were no paved areas for us to ride. We coasted down bumpy hills. We used it to haul feed for the animals. We played with that little red wagon until we wore the wheels off. We repaired the wheels and wore them off again. We finally outgrew it. The last I remember of the wagon, was its battered bed being used as a feeding trough for the chickens.

Of all the many Christmas presents I have received, that present lingers in my mind as one of the most treasured. I shall always remember the Christmas of the little red wagon.

A brief moment in time
William Wayne Dicksion

My Secret Place

I am ten years old. The farm on Spring Creek was situated about two miles from the nearest public road. The trails we used to get to the public roads were two-lane paths across the fields and the prairie. These trails were used by cars, horse-drawn wagons, and buggies. The nearest the mail carrier came to our farm was two miles away. I enjoyed going to get the mail in the summertime. There was a place where the trail crossed Bitter Creek, where there was a beautiful pond in the bend of the creek, with a big elm tree shading the pond. Some of the roots of the tree had been exposed by water erosion. There was a little meadow in the bend of the creek, where wild flowers grew in profusion. The meadow was a place for prairie birds, meadow larks, and rabbits. The water was clear in the pond, and I could see fish such as perch, bass, bluegill, catfish, and brightly colored minnows.

The trees abounded with squirrels. I liked to lie down on the soft grass in the shade, with my head resting on the roots of the big, old elm tree and watch the little, white gulf clouds passing the opening in the branches. Watching them this way gave them definition and motion. I was not lazy, but I was a dreamer. This spot gave me a moment of respite from the trouble and turmoil of my everyday life. If I would lie very still, after a while the little animals would come out, and I could watch them playing, just the way nature intended them to.

Oftentimes now, when I am troubled, I go back in my mind to this beautiful spot, and I watch the world the way I perceived the Almighty Creator meant it to be. A peace settles over me and in a while, I can go on and face the world of turmoil around me, with a feeling of a new beginning.

Yes, the creeks of my childhood had a lot to do with who I am today.

A brief moment in time
William Wayne Dicksion

The Railroad Trestle

The railroad passed through Uncle Arthur's farm, which was about two or three miles from our farm. He and Aunty Betty had a large family like our own. Their kids were our cousins. We spent many a Sunday afternoon playing together, getting into all kinds of mischief.

The railroad track provided many opportunities for adventure. We would place nails on the track, and the iron wheels of the train would flatten them out into some interesting shapes. When we placed pennies on the rails, the wheels would roll them out flat as a fritter.

There was a railroad bridge which crossed a deep canyon where the right-of-way crossed my uncle's farm. The bridge had no side rails and no overhead structures, so it was called a trestle. We used to talk about what we would do if we should get caught out on that trestle when the train was coming. If you were in the middle of that bridge when you saw a train coming, you would be trapped. The distance to the end of the bridge was too far to run to get off the trestle before the train would catch you. And it was much too high to jump from the rails into the canyon below. The rail ties did not extend out far enough from the rails to allow the person to stand on them and avoid the train. Someone suggested that it might be possible to hang onto the railroad ties with your hands while the train passed. It would be a mighty risky thing to try.

On a dare, my cousin, Dink, and I said we could do it. Dink was indeed a very daring, young man, and I certainly was not going to let him out-dare me. We waited until we could hear a train coming, then we walked on the ties to the center of the trestle and waited. Soon we could see the train coming. I knew we were committed to carry out our dare. It was too late to get off the trestle before the train would be upon us. By the time the engineer saw us, it was too late for him to stop the train. I looked down and considered jumping onto the boulders. It was a long way down. It only took me a second to change my mind about that alternative. Dink and I both climbed out on the ties and swung down, holding on with just our hands. The engineer on the train was going crazy! He was pulling that whistle with all his might! I had never heard such a racket. It was a very exciting time, looking down at the boulders way down there, then looking up at a wailing, roaring, freight train bearing down on us with no possible chance of stopping.

The train instantly was passing over us. I had never realized how much dirt, dust, and debris would fall off a freight train, or how much the trestle would shake with the train passing.

We waited and waited for the train to pass; it must have been a mile long. My hands were getting very tired, but there was no choice. There was nothing left to do but hang on. I closed my eyes and concentrated on just hanging on. I opened them just long enough to look at Dink—his eyes were closed also. After what seemed like an eternity, the train passed.

Now, the question in my mind was, *Do I have enough strength to pull myself back up to the rails?* After struggling, I made it. I was just lying there on the rails, shaking like a leaf. Dink was lying on the rails nearby. He, too, was in a state of shock.

The other kids came running up to us all laughing and shouting. According to them, we were heroes. I did not feel like a hero. I felt kinda stupid. I was thinking, *I will never do a thing like that again.*

Anyway, the praise did not last long. We were off to the next wild and exciting adventure; running on the creek, fishing, swimming, and hunting animals. Then we had chores to do, which were a necessary part of living on a farm.

Our parents would occasionally catch us doing some of the crazy things. We expected to get whippings from time to time, and that we did, but it sure did not daunt our spirits much.

A brief moment in time
William Wayne Dicksion

The Wisdom of the Old Indian

There was an old Indian man who lived in the woods, all alone, in a small, one-room cabin with a dirt floor. The cabin was built of a mixture of logs, hides, and mud. The cabin had a fireplace, and some wall hangings which consisted of animal skins, and tools he used around the cabin. There was a big, black, iron pot and a heavy, iron skillet hanging from pegs by the fireplace. I don't know how old he was, but to me, he seemed ancient. He was alone, but he didn't seem lonely. He just didn't seem to need anyone. He must have had some friends or family, but I never saw anyone except the old Indian man at his cabin.

His face was craggy and wrinkled. I almost never saw him smile or frown. His eyes were dark and deep-set. He didn't seem to look at you; he seemed to look right through you. There was nothing sinister or evil looking about him. He just looked different. I remember thinking, *He is very old, and must know just about everything there is to know about the woods, the animals, and the land. I sure would like to talk to him. I would like to learn what he knows.*

One day, while I was on one of my long, exploring walks into the woods, which I liked to make after I had completed my chores on the farm, I walked near the old Indian's cabin. I could see by the smoke coming from his chimney that he was home. I had gathered some wild persimmons. I thought if I offered some of the fruit to him, he might talk to me.

I went to the opening of his cabin. It wasn't really a door; it was just an opening, with an old, striped blanket hanging to one side that could be released. When the blanket was hanging loose, it served as a door. I knocked on one of the logs near the opening and called out, "Hello." I could see him sitting inside, but he did not respond to my call. I stuck my head in and asked, "May I come in?" He still didn't show any signs that would indicate that he had heard me. He didn't say 'yes' but he didn't say 'no', either. I stepped inside, extended the hand holding the wild persimmons, and asked if he would like some. He took his eyes off mine just long enough to look at the wild fruit I was offering. He did not reach out to accept the fruit, so I lay it down beside him. He still did not reach for the fruit; he probably just did not know what to make of me, a white boy, offering him a gift. Perhaps he was wondering what he could give in exchange.

My father had told me, for an Indian to accept a gift, he must give something in return. I sat down in front of him with my legs crossed the way his legs were crossed. He then handed me a small piece of wood with some carving on it. I did not know then and I don't know now what it was, but it must have been something which he valued. After I had accepted the gift, he then reached for one of the persimmons and ate it. He did not offer me one, but I had already eaten all I wanted. When he had finished eating the persimmon, he looked at me and made a sound deep in his throat, and I concluded that was a signal that the visit was over. I got up, said goodbye and left. He said nothing, just watched me go with those all-knowing eyes. I had committed several social errors and done some things that I felt sure my parents would not approve of. I thought it best if I just kept the whole thing a secret. I was sorry there had been no opportunity for me to ask him any of the many questions I wanted to ask. I had to get home. It was time to milk the cows and feed the animals.

A couple of weeks later, one of our turkey hens was missing. Dad said that she was probably nesting, and he told me to go find her. He said that if I could find her nest, I would find her. We did not keep our animals penned up. They were healthier if they ran wild and they could forage for their own food. Turkeys like to hide their nests. A turkey hen will not go far from her nest; she has to guard her eggs. There are many things in the wild that like to eat eggs, such as possums, snakes, pigs, and even straying dogs or coyotes. A turkey hen is quite capable of driving off any of these predators.

While hunting for the turkey's nest, I found myself near the old Indian's cabin. He was sitting outside this time, and he was chewing on some meat he had preserved by smoking it.

He lived entirely off the land. He had no garden, nor did he raise any farm animals like cows, chicken and pigs. He just didn't seem to need them. He lived only on what nature provided. When I was in his cabin before, I did not see a gun. I hadn't even seen a bow and arrow, so that meant that whatever meat he ate, he had to trap it. I sure wanted to know what he knew about trapping animals, and the other things he must know about living in the woods.

As I was walking by, he held up his hand in a gesture to me. I walked over to see what he wanted. He offered me a piece of the meat he was chewing. All I had to give him in return were three glass marbles that I happened to have in my pocket. I always carried a pocketknife, but I didn't want to give that up. He seemed pleased with the exchange, so I sat down near him and began chewing on the meat. It was surprisingly good.

I asked, "What kind of meat are we eating?"

He spoke for the first time, and in pretty good English. Anyway, it was pretty good Oklahoma English, and that was the language I understood.

He said. "We are eating rabbit."

"Would you show me what kind of arrow you used to shoot the rabbit?"

He smiled for the first time. It was almost a laugh. I knew that, to him, I had asked a foolish question.

He answered, "You don't use an arrow to shoot a rabbit. That would be a waste of a good arrow. Do you know how long it takes to make a good arrow?"

I admitted, "No, I don't. My brothers and I make bows and arrows to play with, but they are not good enough to hunt with. If you did not use an arrow to shoot the rabbit, then how did you get the rabbit that we are eating?"

He answered me by asking a question. "What does a rabbit do if you scare it from its hiding place?"

"It runs."

"And what does it do if you run after it?"

"It runs into a hole." I replied.

"Then make a hole for it to run into," he said. Then he asked, "What kind of hole is the rabbit's favorite hiding place?"

"A hollow log."

"Then make a hollow log for the rabbit to run into."

"How do you do that?"

He explained, "When you have found a hollow log that would be a suitable hiding place for a rabbit, cut a piece of wood out of the top of the hollow log so you can reach into the log and grasp the rabbit which is trapped in the log."

"What is to stop the rabbit from escaping by running out the same hole he ran into?"

He continued with his explanation, "Sharpen the end of sticks made from the branches of a willow tree. The small sticks will be flexible. Place the sharpened sticks in a cone shape around the opening in the end of the log, with the sharp ends of the sticks pointing in and forming the small end of the cone, pointing to the inside of the log. Everything about your trap is made of natural things that the rabbit is used to, and there is nothing to frighten him. So the rabbit will not hesitate to run into the log. He can easily push the thin sticks aside as he goes into the log, but when he tries to get out the sharpened ends of the sticks will poke him. He will not struggle against it because he does not feel threatened. He doesn't want to hurt himself on the sharpened sticks, so he sits quietly in the log until you are ready to open the door at the top, reach in, and get the rabbit. When you put the door back in the opening you had cut into the top of the log, your trap is set for the next rabbit."

I was amazed at the simplicity of the trap and the just common-sense thinking involved in the making of it. Now, this is the kind of knowledge I wanted to get from this remarkable, old man. I didn't want to stay too long and wear out my welcome. I wanted to be able to come back. There were so many questions I wanted answers to.

"I must go now. May I come back? I want you to teach me some of the things you know about living in the woods."

He looked at me with a deep, questioning look and asked, "Why do you want to know?"

"I have heard my parents and grandparents talking. They say that the old ways are dying, and most of the truths of how it was are being lost. I want to preserve the knowledge, so I can tell my children and grandchildren what you teach me."

"How are you going to keep the information?"

"I will keep it the same way you have kept it. I will remember."

He said, "No one is going to believe stories told by a mere boy."

"I will wait until I am no longer a boy before I tell the stories. I will wait until I am an old man, and after the truths of what you tell me have been forgotten, I will tell them again for anyone who wants to know."

He seemed satisfied with my answer. He nodded to me; I nodded in return, got up from where I was sitting, and left.

After I left, I couldn't stop thinking about the simple beauty of what he had told me. Then I remembered why I was out in the woods in the first place. I was looking for a turkey nest. I wondered if I could think like the old Indian. *Would it help me to find the turkey's nest?* So I tried to think like a turkey. *If I were a turkey, where would I hide my nest? I would build my nest on a high spot where I could see if a predator was coming my way.* Building the nest on a high spot would prevent it from being washed away should there be a big rain. I would need to build the nest among tall grass to keep the nest hidden. I would want it to be near water so I could get a drink and not have to leave the nest exposed to predators for too long. I am giving that ol' turkey a lot of credit for intelligence. I had always been told that turkeys are pretty dumb birds, but I wanted to try it the way I thought the old Indian would try it.

What did I have to loose; I wasn't finding the nest my way. So I started looking for knolls of grass near water. In less than an hour I found the nest. I wondered, *Was it just a coincidence?*

I went home and told my father that I had found the nest. He said he was wondering what was taking me so long. He was pleased that I had found the nest. He told me to keep an eye on the nest so I would know when the little turkeys had hatched. We could then bring them into the barn and raise them for the benefit of the farm. That was perfect. It gave me an excuse for being away from the farm and I would be able to learn more from my new friend. I hoped I had made a new friend.

I went back to see the Indian several times, and we talked about many things. He taught me how to build a stick trap for birds, and how to build a warm shelter if I were ever caught out in a blizzard. He taught me how to make a really good bow and arrow, to use for hunting, or to be used as a weapon if the need should ever arise.

He said, "Never use a weapon in anger. A weapon used in anger is as bad for the one using it, as it is for the one it is being used against." He said he thought that anger was the main reason the Indians failed so miserably in their struggle with the white man for the control of the land. The land is what the struggle was all about. The white man wanted to own the land. The Indians believed that no one should own the land. The Indian destroyed himself with his own anger. If the Indian and the white man had learned to live together, both would have benefited.

I was too young to understand what he was trying to tell me.

He taught me to catch fish with green walnuts, and how to empty the ponds in the creeks. By draining the ponds, you could get all the fish you wanted. You just had to know how to drain the ponds.

He said, "Listen to the birds and the animals, and they will tell you when there is danger near. Be very quiet so the animals will not be afraid. They will come out from where they are hiding, and you can watch and learn from them. The animals will talk to you, if you will just learn to listen. There is much they can teach you."

Not long after that visit, my family moved to another part of the state. I never saw my old friend again. I have always felt a great loss. He had a wisdom that I wish our statesmen of today had a little of. There is another great struggle going on and we need men of wisdom to solve the problems, so that all mankind can live together in peace.

I never knew the old Indian's name—no names were ever used. I later learned that there had been an old Indian man who had lived there who was called Gray Eagle.

A brief moment in time
William Wayne Dicksion

The Creeks of My Childhood

The children I grew up with knew little of the lives of children who grew up in the cities. We would hear them talking of their territory, their street, their block, their school, their turf. We knew nothing of these things. For us it was the creeks. We never thought of them as "our creeks." The creeks belonged to everyone, as far as kids were concerned. Even though the creek ran through another farmer's land, nobody cared if we waded in the creek, swam in the creek, or fished in the creek. And most people did not care if we hunted along the creek. The creeks ran from property to property; the water belonged to no one. The fish in the streams swam up and down the creeks. The rabbits ran from property to property. The birds flew wherever they wanted to go. They were as free as the wind, and we were as free as the birds, when we played on the creeks.

It was an enchanting way to grow up. Around every bend in the creek was a new pond of water. There was a place to swim, or fish, or just play in the shade of the big, old trees. We looked for bird nests, watched little squirrels playing in the trees, and rabbits playing in the fields. We would watch the birds building their nests and feeding their young. I remember the sounds of the creeks: the tinkling sounds of the little streams as they ran from pond to pond, the fish splashing in the pools, the squirrels chattering, the meadow larks sitting on fence posts singing their hearts out. I remember walking under the trees, looking up, and watching the branches of the trees dancing in the wind.

We were a part of all of this, and all of this was a part of us. Wouldn't it be wonderful if every child could grow up on a creek?

Children can learn more while growing up on one of those creeks than they will learn from all the books they will ever read. They can learn the beauty and symmetry of life being displayed in full color right before their eyes. They learn of mating, of birthing, of a mother's love, the suckling, the tending, the caring, and the young growing to adulthood. Then they learn the sorrow and the beauty of growing old and dying.

We would witness the deathlike cold of winter when the trees were all silent, stark and bare. The ponds of the little streams would be frozen. We would wonder what happened to the fish that had lived in that pond. The birds were quiet. The squirrels were hidden and silent.

Oh, the long wait. Then one day, a warm beam of sunlight breaks through the gray, winter clouds and shines on the meadow in the bend of the creek. A small piece of green pokes its way up through the soil and in what seems like only a moment, the whole creek springs to life. Spring has come. Life has returned to the creeks of my childhood. The child returns to play along the creek, one year older, and a lifetime wiser.

That child has witnessed a moment in eternity. I know now that I had witnessed the life force of the universe in action. From what book can you gain that knowledge? That was a part of growing up in poverty stricken, dust-bowl Oklahoma. No prince or princess ever grew up in greater splendor. Oh, if every child could grow up on a creek.

A brief moment in time
William Wayne Dicksion

Snowball

I was walking home from where the school bus had dropped me off. It was still more than a mile to our farmhouse. I don't know how cold it was, but the puddles of water along the wagon trail were frozen. There was a cold wind blowing, causing the barbed wires of the pasture fence to make a humming sound. I had the earflaps of my winter cap pulled down and tied under my chin. My ears were still cold. I wanted to rub my ears, but I was afraid to rub them as they might fall off. I had cotton gloves on my hands and my hands stuffed into my jacket pockets. They were still cold.

Above the howl of the wind, I heard a tiny sound. I stopped to listen. It had sounded like the mewing of a baby kitten. Nah, that couldn't be. Not out here on the prairie in this kind of weather. I started to move on. There, I heard it again! It was coming from what looked like a bundle of rags laying in a gully. I crawled into the gully to take a look. I heard it again, very faintly, but I heard it. The sound was definitely coming from what looked like an old flour sack that someone had thrown into the gully. There was a drawstring at the mouth of the sack. I opened the sack and looked inside.

A mother cat and her litter of baby kittens had been tossed into the gulley to get rid of them. They were all dead but one tiny kitten. It was so white, it looked like a snowball laying there wrapped in those rags. The little, white kitten was almost dead. I picked it up and put it inside my jacket to keep it warm. I didn't know what I was going to do with it, but I couldn't leave it there in that gully to die. Somehow, I was not as cold, now that I was concerned about keeping the kitten warm.

When I walked into our farmhouse, there was a fire in the wood-burning stove in the center of the living room. I walked to the stove to get warm. My mother was busy in the kitchen preparing supper for the family, but she was never too busy to check on her family. She came into the living room to check on me.

The first thing she said was, "What have you got under your jacket?" How could she notice that I had something under my jacket? The kitten was so small I didn't think anyone would notice it.

I reached inside my jacket and removed the kitten. Mother took it into her hands with a sad look on her face, shook her head, and said, "It sure is a pretty little thing, but it is too young to survive without its mother's milk. Where did you find it?"

I related the story of my finding the kitten. Mother said, "I am pleased that you have a good heart and want to save its life, but I am afraid it is hopeless. I suggest you take it out into the field and bury it."

"Mom, I can't do that. It is still alive and I sure can't kill it and then bury it. May I try to save it?"

"How will you feed it?"

"We have eyedroppers. I could heat cow's milk, warm it just enough to make it like its mother's milk, and feed the kitten with an eyedropper."

"Son, I don't think it will work, but if you want to try, I will help you all I can. You know that if you are successful and manage to get it to live, you will not be able to keep it in the house after it is old enough to run around. Your father has a rule; no animals inside the house. I will talk to him and see if he will let you keep it in the house until you can get it old enough to live on its own in the barn. He may not even let you keep it in the barn. The rule on the farm is everything must earn its own keep. How can a cat pay its own way?"

"It could catch mice which are always in the granary."

"Yes, that is a possibility. If you can convince your father to give it a try, then it is all right with me. Now get that cat taken care of. You have chores to do before supper, and then you have your homework to do before you can go to sleep. You had better get busy."

I took the kitten to the barn where I milked one of the cows and while the milk was still warm from the cow, I gave some of the milk to the kitten. The kitten didn't want to take the milk from the eyedropper at first, but after trying again and again the kitten began hungrily taking the milk. After feeding the kitten, I put it back inside my jacket to keep it warm, and it was soon fast asleep.

I knew my parents would never allow me to take the kitten to bed with me, so I borrowed my mother's hot water bottle, wrapped it in some cloth, put the kitten in a bed I made for it from a cardboard box, and placed it beside my bed. I had to get up twice during the night to feed the kitten.

The next morning I had to go to school. Mother said she would take care of the kitten while I was in school.

As time passed, the kitten kept getting stronger and stronger, until one day my father said, "Son, that cat is old enough to make it on his own. Take it to the barn and see if it will catch those mice."

This next step was the crucial test. It would determine the fate of the cat. If it caught some of the mice, it would be allowed to stay. If it did not, I would have to get rid of it.

We watched it closely. The first three days it caught no mice. Father did not say anything, but I could see by the look on his face that he was becoming skeptical.

I asked my older brother what I should do.

"Are you feeding the cat?" he asked.

"Yes, I am feeding it just like I always have."

"Then quit feeding it. Mice are food for cats. If it gets hungry enough, it will catch the mice for food."

The next day Snowball came to me crying for food. I told him, "No. Go catch your own food."

On the third day of going without food, we saw the cat catching a mouse.

My father had a smile on his face, and I knew that Snowball had a place on the farm.

Snowball became my closest friend. He would walk with me to catch the school bus, and he would be waiting for me when the bus brought me home. He would follow me when I went into the pasture to get the cows to bring them in to be milked. He liked to ride with me in the saddle when I rode a horse to bring in the cattle.

Years passed. I was becoming a young man and Snowball was getting old. We were still steadfast friends. World War II came and I had to leave the farm.

When I returned years later, Snowball was gone, but there was a litter of baby kittens on the neighbor's farm. One of the kittens was as white as snow. Snowball had left his mark. I felt a little better.

A brief moment in time
William Wayne Dicksion

The Rough Riders and the Haunted House

The time was early December, 1934. Almost everyone was desperately poor. There were many abandoned farms and empty houses. Many of the people had moved on. Some went to California; some went to the industrialized cities of the northeast and the great lakes, trying to find a place where they could start over, rebuild their lives, and provide for their families. A few hardy souls were trying to hang on and struggle through the rough times.

Dink, Tyre, Milt, Drew and Joe were the sons of some of these hardy people. These five boys formed a band who played together when they were not too busy working on their parents' farms and helping out with their families' businesses. The boys called their group, "The Rough Riders." The name was taken from Teddy Roosevelt's famous brigade who charged up San Juan Hill in Cuba, during the Spanish-American War.

This was a time before radio, television, computers, and movie theaters. If people were going to be entertained, they had to find ways to entertain themselves. The land in which they lived was undeveloped; a land of trees and grass, and for the most part, it was empty. There were no places of commercial entertainment, but for a group of boys, there was much to do. There were creeks, canyons, hills, and valleys to be explored. There were wild animals to hunt, and creeks, ponds and lakes in which they could swim and fish. There were endless trails on which to ride their ponies.

The Rough Riders would organize their activities in advance. They called their escapades, "adventuring."

The night was cold. Just a sliver of a moon could be seen through the thin layer of clouds that went scurrying past. The biting wind was blowing across the prairie, producing a hissing sound as it passed through the bare stems of the weeds and grass. The dry branches of the bushes and shrubs, brushing against their pant legs and boots, created a rasping sound as they walked along.

The boys were all walking along in silence, following a trail that had been made by cattle. They were all very different in character and nature, but they made a good group. Dink, the oldest, a dark haired, dark eyed, wiry kid about 12 years old, was their leader. Dink was not his real name; it was just a nickname they had given him. He looked like he probably had some Indian ancestry. He had a great imagination and was always thinking of interesting things to do. All of the boys liked him. He made a good leader.

Tyre was a gentle boy who loved animals. He always brought his dog along with him on these adventures. Joe, being the youngest at nine years old, was small for his age. But he was a rough-and-tumble kid who could keep up with the best of them. Drew, the biggest of the bunch, was a very stable kinda kid, slow to anger. Milt was the tallest. He was a little timid, being raised by his old-maid aunt. She ran a shop in the little town nearby, so he was what they called a city kid. He had only recently come to live with his aunt. The country life was new to him, but he was game to try any-thing, and he could be depended on when the chips were down.

The boys loved to go adventuring, and this night the adventure was to visit the haunted house. The haunted house was a place which no one in his right mind would want to go, especially on a cold, dark night, with the wind howling across the prairie, making the trip much less than pleasant. Nobody was making any pretense of being in their right mind.

Dink had put out a dare. He dared the boys to go with him and sit in the haunted house, to see if it really was haunted. Each of the boys had to prove to himself that he was not afraid to go at night into the haunted house and see if the house was, or was not, haunted. None of the boys really wanted to go, but if they didn't go, they would be admitting to themselves they were afraid, and they sure didn't want to admit that. None of them wanted to be con-sidered a coward by the rest of the group, so each boy had to call Dink's dare.

Each of them was carrying some article of food they planned to eat after heating it over the fire which they were going to build on the dirt floor of the haunted house. The old house had a fireplace, but they could not sit around a fireplace; they wanted open fire. One of the boys had brought along some wieners and marshmallows. Joe had biscuits which his mother had made. Maybe it wouldn't be so cold after they got inside the old house and got a fire going.

The haunted house was located in the valley of a little stream. Before they got to the old house, they could see it, just a dim outline sitting back among the trees. It was just a dark shadow, old, deserted and cold. It had been abandoned for a long time. The yard had all grown up in weeds. The old scrub oak trees were overhanging the house. The branches were dragging on the roof, making a scratching sound as they rubbed against the handmade shingles. It was the dreariest looking place you could ever imagine.

The only thing they had for a light was a kerosene lantern. The lantern didn't give off much light, but it was better than nothing. Dink, being the leader of the group, was carrying the lantern. He walked up to the old door which was hanging on rusty hinges, and gave it a push. The sound of that door opening was enough to make everyone want to go home. The hinges squeaked. It had been a long time since those hinges had moved. The bottom of the door dragged on the dirt floor. That old house was darker than the inside of a cave at midnight.

The boys were all standing at the now open door, trying to see into the gloomy interior. All they could see, with the feeble light being given off by that old lantern, was some handmade, broken-down furniture, and some worn-out pots and pans lying around on the floor near the fireplace.

Tyre had his dog on a leash. The dog was whining and trying to pull away. Not even the dog wanted to go inside that old house. That did not bode well. The boys all thought that dog wasn't afraid of anything physical, but he was sure afraid of something in that old house.

Dink, while holding the lantern up as high as he could, trying to see inside the house, said, "Well, who's going in with me?"

Drew, who was the next craziest in the bunch, said, "You go first and I'll follow."

The rest of the boys very cautiously followed them in. The house had an eerie feeling about it. It was sure no place you would want to spend the night alone, or with a group, for that matter.

Milt (that was short for Milton) suggested, "Let's get a fire going in here, maybe it will cheer the place up a bit."

Joe said, "I agree. This place needs more than a bit of cheering up, but I'm all for getting a fire going. It is colder than a witch's heart in here."

Dink remarked, "Let's go outside and get some wood for a fire."

There were plenty of deadwood which had fallen from the trees over the years, but it was so dark, they had to feel around with their feet to find it.

"We got enough now," Joe said. "Let's take it inside and see if we can get it to burn."

They finally got a fire going, and it did help a bit. The fire was casting moving shadows on the walls. The dog was nervous and wanted to go outside. Tyre was trying to calm his dog. Everyone was busy getting the food ready to cook.

Everything seemed okay in the house, and Joe asked, "Why do they say this house is haunted?"

Dink answered, "There was a family lived here once, a long time ago. The man was bitten by a rabid dog. There was no cure for the rabies, and the man knew he would go mad. He did not wish to harm any of his family when he went mad, so he chained himself to a post in that other room over there. They say he put a lock on the chain and swallowed the key, so none of his family could unlock him. He did go mad, and after a time, died a horrible death. In his madness, before he died, he struggled against the chains. After he died, the family moved away, never to return. They say the house is haunted because, at times, you can still hear the chains rattling from the mad man struggling, trying to break them."

Without warning, the dog began running around and around the room, barking and howling. It seemed out of its mind. The boys couldn't catch it and they couldn't calm it. After a while, it ran out of the house and off into the woods, still barking and howling.

Drew asked, "Tyre, what's wrong with your dog?"

Tyre replied, "Aw, he is just a pup, and pups have running fits sometimes. Dad says he probably has worms."

Milt asked, "Are you sure he hasn't got rabies?"

Tyre said, "Nah. I'm not sure, but I don't think so."

The boys were starting to get warm from the fire, and from being inside the house, out of the wind.

Joe said, "Let's eat."

They all cut some sticks with their pocketknives and stuck some wieners on the ends of the sticks so they could cook them over the fire. They roasted some marshmallows, using the sticks to hold them over the fire. The food smelled good. The old house was feeling a lot better. They were just sitting around the fire, eating the hot food, and talking about the man being chained in the other room. They were laughing about people thinking they had heard chains rattling in the old, abandoned house.

The fire was starting to die down. The shadows were getting hazy against the walls, looking like grotesque figures moving about the room. No one wanted to go get more wood for the fire. They were just waiting for Tyre's dog to come back. Tyre said, "The dog will come back when he gets over the fit."

Milt asked, "Tyre, why don't you just call that dog?"

Tyre said, in his lisping voice, "I would call that jot damn dog, but I'm afraid he would come."

Everyone was laughing at the humor of Tyre's statement, when all of a sudden, they heard the sound of rattling chains coming from the other room. No one said a word. They looked at each other. The house got very quiet. All they could hear was the moaning sound of the wind blowing around the eaves of the old house, the scratching sound of the tree branches rubbing against the roof, and the pounding of their own hearts like drumbeats in their temples. The moaning of the wind made a sound like that of a mad man in pain.

Dink said, "Ah, that's just the wind." No one replied, just a kind of nodding of their heads, but there was doubt in their eyes.

The moaning sound continued. Then again, without warning, they heard the sound of rattling chains.

"Let's get outta here," cried Milt.

A blast of wind hit the front door, slamming it shut. The door was jammed against the frame. The sound of chains was coming from the other room. It seemed to be getting closer and closer to where the boys were now trapped in the semi-darkened room. They were pulling frantically at the door, but it wouldn't budge.

Joe yelled, "Where in the heck is the back door?"

"We're going to have to find it!" Dink yelled back from the now darkened room.

They were all frantically feeling around the walls for the door which they felt sure would be there somewhere.

Drew called out, "Here it is, and I got it open!"

They all bailed out of that house like it was on fire. They just stood around outside the building, trying to regain their composure. Each of them was looking at that spooky, old house. No one knew what to say. They couldn't figure out what had just happened.

None of them could hear the sounds of chains anymore. No one seemed to know what to do. They had left all of their stuff in the house when they ran out so fast. The dog came back. It was still whining and wanted to get away from the house. No one petted it.

After a while, Dink said, "I've just got to know what is making that rattling sound, and I've got to get my lantern. Who will go back in with me?"

The rest of the boys were thinking, *You've got to be crazy! Who would go back into that house after what we just experienced?*

Nobody was speaking up in reply to Dink's question.

The silence was deafening.

Dink looked at Joe and asked, "Joe, how about you, will you go back in with me?"

Joe had a reputation of never taking a dare–Joe was thinking, *I'm not real bright.* He was trapped. Nobody would blame him if he didn't go, but if Dink was willing to go back in, and Joe refused, then he would have to admit to himself that he was not as brave as Dink. There was no way he was going to admit that.

"OK, let's go," Joe said reluctantly. He was hoping Dink would change his mind.

Now Dink wasn't real bright either, so in they went. They could see the glow of the lantern still sitting in the middle of the room where they had left it. It gave off very little light. All that was left of the fire was some glowing embers which did little to light the old place. It just made it look even spookier.

Joe had a little camper's ax in his hand which he always carried with him when they went on these trips. The ax came in handy when they were building campfires. Joe had no idea what he was going to do with it, going back into that haunted house, but it gave him a feeling of comfort.

When he and Dink got to the door of the bedroom, they stopped and just listened. After a moment, they heard the sound of rattling chains again. There was no doubt this time. That was the sound of rattling chains!

Joe and Dink were caught. To go back was to admit that they did not have the courage to go on with what they had started. But to go on was not something either of them wanted to do. Dink looked at Joe. Joe nodded his head and in they went. At first, they could see nothing. Then, after their eyes adjusted to the dark, they could see something moving in the corner of the room. It was small. It was real. It was no ghost!

Joe moved forward with his ax at the ready. He was moving very cautiously. Then he saw a full-grown opossum, with one of its hind legs caught in a steel trap. The chain was still attached to the trap. Whenever the opossum moved, the chain would rattle.

When the opossum had been caught, it had managed to pull the stake from the ground which held the trap. The stake was supposed to hold the animal till the owner of the trap came to collect whatever the trap had caught. The opossum was now living in the old house and was dragging the trap wherever it went. The opossum was old and had been living in the house for a long time. The house made a perfect den for the injured animal.

Joe asked Dink to hold the animal while he opened the trap, freeing the opossum's leg. The leg had been broken when the trap snapped closed, but it had healed. Now the opossum, after being freed from the steel trap, could move around without having to drag the trap and chain with it. Both Joe and Dink felt good about the opossum, but they were a little sad because they had ruined a perfectly good haunted house.

Joe said to Dink, "Let's don't tell the boys what we found." Dink grinned and just nodded his head. They picked up their stuff from the room where they had left it and joined the boys outside.

Tyre asked, "What did you find?"

Dink said, "All we found was an old opossum living in that other room." Joe nodded his head in agreement.

"Is that all?"

"Yeah, that's all. If you don't believe us, go look for yourselves."

"I'll take your word for it," said Tyre. They could tell by the way he said it that he felt there was more to the story than what was being told, but he was in no mood to go back into that dark, old house and check it out.

They all started home. No one was talking. They were engaged in their own thoughts about what had happened that evening. They never talked much about it after that. They had other places to explore, other adventures to live.

The Rough Riders rode on!

A brief moment in time
William Wayne Dicksion

The Prairie Fire

My two older brothers and I were out one cold winter day hunting fur-bearing animals. Catching these animals and preparing their hides as pelts was how we earned money to spend for things that we might need. This was also a way for us to get a little money to spend for Christmas.

It was very cold. We were out on the prairie. The wind was howling across the hills and gullies. There was no wood with which to build a fire. Tassels of grass had blown into a small gully. We thought, *If we could set the grass tassels on fire, we could get warm.* One of us threw a lighted match into the gully that had blown full of the tassels. The tassels were so dry and burned so quickly, they exploded almost as if we had thrown a match into gasoline. In an instant the fire sprang up and burning tassels of grass blew onto the meadow grass, and the prairie was on fire!

A prairie fire is a very serious thing. They burn so fast and can burn for miles. A prairie fire can do enormous damage. We had made a bad mistake.

I was nine years old. My brothers were 11 and 13. We were very young, but we were country wise and we knew that we were in serious trouble. The fire was burning between the forks of two canyons. We hoped that if we could fight the fire back into the forks of those two canyons, we could control it. The only things we had to fight the fire with were our coats and some green bushes, which we cut with our pocketknives. We fought that fire all afternoon. Now I understand the term, "busy as fighting fire."

Finally, we managed to contain it into the fork in the canyons. The strategy had worked and we extinguished the fire. We were bone tired. Our hair and eyebrows were singed. Our clothes were smudged and torn. Our faces and hands were burned and red. We had not had a drink of water all day. We must have looked a mess when we walked into the house.

When our mother saw us she asked, "What on earth happened to you?"

After we explained, Dad just gave us an all-knowing look and said as he walked away, "Well, I guess you learned a lesson. Come on, we've got to go milk the cows and do the chores."

Nothing, absolutely nothing, could get in the way of milking those damn cows.

A brief moment in time
William W. Dicksion

First Day in a New School

The year was 1935. We, like most farming families in Oklahoma at that time, were poor. We were tenant farmers and leased the land from owners who usually lived somewhere else. The leases were yearly leases. These short-term leases made it necessary for us to move every year or two.

The owner of the last farm from which we had moved decided he wanted to move onto his own land. He and my father terminated their lease agreement, and we moved to our present farm. This new farm was a much better farm. It had better land, better grass, and a beautiful stream running through it. The stream was called Spring Creek.

The low, rambling farmhouse sat surrounded by stately oak trees. The house sat on a bluff overlooking the valley of Spring Creek. The bluff on which the house was built was located about fifty feet from the south side of the house. The bluff was about twenty feet high. There were also oak and elm trees growing along the edge of the bluff, and they provided shade during the summer. Some previous occupant had tied a three-quarter-inch steel cable high on a branch of one of the trees, and had tied a sack of straw to the end of the cable, creating a swing. We could, by holding onto the cable and by wrapping our legs around the sack of straw, ride the long, swinging arc from the knoll, out over the stream, and drop into a pool of water, which was created by the stream as it flowed along the bottom of the bluff. It was a wonderful place to play, and in the summer, when it was warm enough to swim, it was even better.

It was now autumn. The soft, warm, summer nights, with the sounds of night birds calling and the flickering light of fireflies dancing in the gloom, were gone, and the nights were getting cold. We will have to wait until next year, when the weather gets warm, before we can again enjoy the swing and the swimming hole under it.

For me, this was the day I had been dreading for weeks. It was to be my first day at the new school. It was not only the first day of school, it was the first day of school at a <u>new</u> school. First days at new schools were always difficult. You have to get acquainted with your new teachers, make new friends, and you always have to fight the bully at the new school. I was not afraid of the bully, and I didn't mind the fighting so much, it was just that the fighting didn't really prove anything. I didn't like the spankings I always got from the school principles and the whipping I got from my father when I got home. I just wished it didn't have to be done.

I had to walk about four or five miles across prairie land laced with hills and gullies. The prairie had small, tree-lined creeks running through it, where the water had cut away the dirt and left the red clay banks of the stream exposed. In the bends of the creek, there were pools of water with brightly colored minnows darting around, gathering the mosquito larva and other small insects that happened to land in the pools.

It took me more than an hour to walk the distance. There were no roads; just trails that had been made by horse-drawn wagons.

The sun was just rising over the horizon. There were a few clouds in the pale blue, morning sky. It was going to be a warm September day. I could smell the autumn in the air. The grass no longer had a vibrant, green color. The tips of the leaves were turning brown.

The cattle were just starting to graze; they looked at me as I walked by, and seemed surprised to see me.

I carried my lunch in a one-gallon, cane syrup pail. My lunch consisted of a homemade flour biscuit, with a piece of fried pork between the slices, and a couple of shortbread cookies. I had a pad of lined paper and a lead pencil. I did not have books, because I did not know what books I would need.

I spent every summer going without shoes, so I was going to school barefoot. I was wearing a pair of blue-bibbed over-alls, and a shirt that had belonged to my older brother. He had not quite worn it out, so it had passed on to me. I was wearing a straw hat that was a bit frazzled around the brim. My father had cut my hair yesterday. I should have combed it while it was wet, but I didn't get to it until after it had dried, so now it was flying off in all directions when I removed my hat. I had scrubbed clean, but I was a sorry-looking sight, and I knew it.

I was not looking forward to meeting all of the new people. I wasn't feeling good about how I looked, and I was wondering what my new school would be like.

I hurried across the rolling countryside. I didn't want to be late for my first day at the new school.

The school was a one-story, brick building that sprawled across the top of a low hill. It was big for a country school. Dad said, "Many years ago, the area had been a prosperous cattle-raising country. The ranchers built a big school for educating all of their children from grade one to grade twelve. When the area had been prosperous, there was a railroad that ran through the town."

The location had been a loading site for cattle being shipped to the markets back east. There had been large corrals and loading pens for the handling of the cattle. In its heyday, this had been a full-fledged frontier town with stores, saloons, and a house where ladies of the night entertained the single men who worked the cattle for the ranchers. A few years back, the government opened the land for homesteading. The farmers fenced the land, broke the sod, and planted their crops. The rains and the winds came and washed the rich few inches of topsoil off the clay base hills, leaving the land worthless for either farming or grazing. All it would produce now was jackrabbits, coyotes, and rattlesnakes. Most of the ranchers had given up and moved on. The cattle were gone; the clay hills were barren. Many of the farmers had to leave, and the little town died. All that was left was the school, a church that only a few people attended, and some buildings which were falling down. There was one store, which sold school supplies to the students. It was the only business that still remained. The few farmers who had tried to hang on and continue farming the depleted land were all very poor, but there were still enough students to maintain a school. The money to pay the teachers and maintain the school came from the government.

I walked up the stone steps into the redbrick building. After I entered the building, I found myself looking down a long hallway with doors on each side. The first door on the right was a wooden door. The top half of the door was made of frosted glass, with the word "OFFICE" printed on it. I carefully opened the door and looked in. There was a counter, a little too high for me to look over without getting up on my toes. A lady was sitting at a desk on the other side of the counter. I cleared my throat to attract her attention. She looked up with a "What do you want?" look in her eye. When she saw me, the look on her face softened a bit, and she said, "Yeess?"

"Could you tell me how to get to the sixth-grade room?" I asked.

She swung her head to the right, indicating the direction. "It's down the hall, the last door on the left."

The floor of the hall was made of wood that had been oiled. I could smell the oil; it had a slight odor of creosote. I guessed they put oiled sawdust on the floors when they swept to help keep the dust down. That was a common practice in public buildings. It worked, but the bottoms of your feet would get oily if you walked on it with bare feet, which most of the students did, when the weather was warm.

When I got to the last door on my left, I opened it very slowly, with no idea what lay beyond. Sitting at the desk in the front of an empty classroom was a young woman, a little plump, a little prim, and a little pretty, with a very kind face. She was wearing a loose-fitting skirt and blouse. When she looked up and saw me, a smile lit her face and she asked, "Who might you be?"

"My name is Daniel August Duncan. They call me Danny, and I'm in the sixth grade."

"You may call me Miss Pringle. I will be your teacher."

She pointed to the seats to her right and said, "The fifth grade students sit over here and sixth grade students sit there," pointing to the seats on the left side of the room. "Just take a seat. The rest of the children will be along in a little while."

I selected a seat in the first row on the left side of the room. I sat at a desk just three seats back from the front of the class. I didn't want to be right in front, or in the extreme back of the room. I wanted to kinda blend in. There was a blackboard across the front of the room behind the teacher's desk. There were erasers and some white chalk in a tray at the bottom of the blackboard. The desks and seats for the students were made of polished wood. The desktops had slots carved into them to hold pencils. There was an inkwell in the upper left corner. The desktop was made so it would slope slightly toward the student. The seat was hinged so it could be tilted up out of the way for cleaning the floors.

"You can put your lunch pail in the closet. You had better put your name on it," she said, as she handed me a pencil.

That meant that some of the other kids were bringing their lunch to school in a syrup bucket also. I felt a little better about my lunch container.

Miss Pringle said, "If you need to use the toilet, the boys' toilet is the first door on the right side of the hall, just before you go out the back door."

Surely, they don't go to the toilet inside the school building. I gotta see this. I went out in the hall, turned left, and sure enough, there was a door with the word "BOYS" written on it, just inside the back door of the building. I went through the door into the room, and there was a short wall with a passageway to the left, so you could not see into the toilet from the hallway. Behind the wall on one side of the room, there was a row of seats with holes in them, located over openings in the floor. On the other side of the room, there was a metal trough attached to the wall, with a slant in the trough so it would drain to one end. In that end there was a hole for the water to run out. But it didn't run out; it just run into a pipe that extended into the floor. *Now this is a pretty strange place. I can't use this toilet located inside the building.* I decided to wait until I got back out in the prairie, on the way home. This was strange and downright unsanitary.

There were several kids in the classroom when I went back, and one of them was sitting in the seat I had selected, so I took the one in the next row. Miss Pringle just smiled and continued with her paperwork.

In walked two girls. One was skinny, with black hair and black eyes. Her skin was very white. You could see she had been protecting her face from the burning rays of the sun. She had a high, thin nose with a puckered little mouth under it, which she held in a constant, mischievous, little smile. She was kinda pretty. She could have been very pretty if she didn't have that mischievous look on her face.

The other one was not just a girl. I thought she must be an angel. She had blond hair, with long curls hanging down in the back, soft brown eyes that sparkled, and a smile that lit up the room. Everyone was looking at her. She didn't even seem to notice, but I had a feeling that she did notice, and was kinda pleased with all the attention.

The two girls sat in the front seats of the first two rows of the class on the teacher's right-hand side, so that meant they were in the fifth grade. I couldn't keep my eyes off the one with the blond hair. She was the prettiest thing I had ever seen. She caught me looking at her, threw her head back, and looked away. Everything about the act was disdainful. She had thrown her head back so quickly that the curls on the back of her head just kept bouncing. I had been put down, but good. I didn't blame her; I looked terrible. I felt so low, I was thinking, *I would have to look up to say good morning to a snake.* Everybody was looking at me.

Miss Pringle called the class to order and I was glad to get the attention off me. She asked us to stand. We put our hands over our hearts and pledged allegiance to the flag of the United States of America and to the Republic for which it stands, one nation, indivisible, with liberty and justice for all. I didn't know what a Republic was, but it must be very important. Everybody stood for just a moment and looked proud, and then we were asked to be seated.

The teacher took roll call. When she called out a name, a student would stand and say, "Here." She didn't call out my name. She probably didn't remember it. It had been several minutes since I had told her my name.

After roll call, and everybody got settled in their seats, Miss Pringle said, "Class, we have a new student this morning." She looked right at me and said, "Would you come to the front of the class and tell us your name and where you live?"

When she looked at me and called me to come to the front of the class, I was thinking, *Now I know how a rabbit feels when it is trapped inside a hollow log with just no way out.* I remember my father telling me, "Son, always walk proud, with your head up and your shoulders back." I sure didn't feel proud, but I held my head up, put my shoulders back, and walked briskly to the front of the room. *I'll sure be glad to get this over with.*

Miss Pringle looked pleased. The girl with the blond, curly hair and big, brown eyes was looking at me, but she sure showed no admiration. There was just something about that look that made me feel, well, somehow inadequate.

After I completed that long walk to the front of the room, I turned and faced the class and looked them right in the eye, all of them.

"My name is Daniel August Duncan. I live about four or five miles northwest of here, over on Spring Creek." I couldn't tell them my address. Farms don't have no address;

all they got is a location. I nodded my head and said, "Thank you." Then I quickly walked back to my seat, sat down, and heaved a big sigh of relief.

The teacher smiled. The rest of the kids were grinning, all except one, and she was just looking at the blackboard at the front of the room. I already knew, without a doubt, it was going to take a lot to gain her acceptance, but I just gotta do it somehow. She sure is pretty.

The teacher took a book from inside her desk, and all the kids got real quiet. I knew something was going to happen. She started reading. It was a story about a man named Robin, who lived in a place called Sherwood Forest. I had never heard about a place like that. I knew there was a bird named robin but I sure never heard of no man called that. The name sounded a little sissy to me, but all of the kids in the class seemed to like this guy. Robin and his band of merry men were hiding from some bad guy who owned all of the land, and he even owned some of the people. Robin and his men had killed a deer with a bow and arrow. I guessed they were hungry. I figured out right away that they didn't have any guns. They were not supposed to kill the deer, because the bad guy owned the deer also. I had never heard of any such a thing, a man who thought he owned the wild animals. It was easy to see why these people didn't like him and were trying to hide from this crazy man. I realized right away that I had joined the class in the middle of this story, and I was going to have trouble trying to figure it out.

Just when the story was getting good, Miss Pringle stopped reading. She said she would read the next chapter tomorrow. I sure didn't want to wait until tomorrow to find out what happened, but we just had no choice, because it was time for arithmetic class to start.

At ten o'clock, a bell rang and the kids all jumped up and ran outside. All you could hear was the clatter of the kids hurrying to get outside. I asked one of the boys what was happening, and he said it was time for recess. I knew about recess all right, but they had never rang no bell before. I was really glad they rang that bell because I had to use the toilet. I didn't have enough time to run down to the creek. I sure didn't feel right about relieving myself inside the school-house. I went through the door with the name "BOYS" written on it to see what the other boys were doing. They were all lined up at the trough, relieving themselves. I sure didn't want to do it, but I just had no choice. I felt awful guilty about it, but the other kids didn't even seem to think there was anything wrong with what they were doing. After going to the toilet, all the kids were running outside to play. I went with them. I didn't know anybody, and nobody knew me, so I just stood and watched while they played a ball game.

Three boys walked up to me and I knew right away that I was going to be tested to see if I would fight. This was something you had to go through any time you went to a new school. You had to prove that you <u>will</u> fight. You didn't have to fight well, but you had to be willing to fight. If you weren't willing to fight, you were labeled a coward and the other kids would have nothing to do with you. My father knew about this custom and had taught me and my two older brothers how to fight. He had taught us the skill of boxing and the art of wrestling. I was lucky, because most of the kids just knew how to scuffle, which was enough most of the time, but if the tough kid you had to fight was really tough, you sure got beat up on. Usually the fight only lasted a few minutes, and the worst you got was skinned up a bit.

When I looked at the kid in the middle, I knew that he was going to be tough. He had white hair, a freckled face, and pale blue eyes. He had a pug nose. He looked like a pug-nosed bulldog. There was arrogance in his eyes, which said, "I am the toughest kid in school."

He walked right up to me and said, "I am Joe Dully, and I don't like you." The two boys standing on each side of him were glaring at me with their hands on their hips. I knew that if I whipped the one in the middle, I would not have to fight the other two, but if I failed, and I suspected that most kids did fail, I was going to have to fight them, also.

"Well, Joe Dully, my name is Danny Duncan, and I don't care if you like me or not. I don't see much about you to like, and I sure don't see anything about you to be afraid of, so I just don't care if you like me or not."

He had not expected that kind of a reply and at first was taken aback. He just didn't quite know what to say, so he just said, "I am the toughest kid in school, and I am going to whip you."

"Well, I see you brought you some help, but I don't think you have enough. They look like a couple of sissies to me, and you sure are not big enough to do the job by yourself."

I knew that I was not going to have to fight all three of them at the same time. It was against the code of honor and anyone engaging in such conduct would be ostracized by the whole school.

"I suggest you wait until lunch hour if you are going to try to whip me. Recess is about over and you are going to need some time to do this job," I said.

Joe said, "OK, we will wait until the lunch hour and we will settle this then."

He didn't sound quite so sure of himself now. I knew I had the advantage. He would be thinking about it until lunch hour, wondering if he had bitten off more than he could chew.

He was a little bigger than me, but I felt sure I could beat him with the training I had received. I knew that every kid in school would hear about this, and that we were going to have a big audience. The teachers would know about it also, but they wouldn't interfere. It was a rite of passage and they understood it. I suspect they watched from behind curtained windows to make sure no one really got hurt. Bloody noses and black eyes were to be expected. And in a really good contest, they usually occurred.

After the recess period was over, we all returned to the classrooms. Everybody was looking at me. All except the pretty girl with the blond curls and brown eyes—she was glaring at me.

Then I remembered. When Miss Pringle called the roll, this girl answered to the name of Rebecca Dully. The bully I've got to fight at lunchtime is her brother! This is a no-win situation. I am sure not going to make friends with her by whipping her brother, and I feel sure I can whip him. Now, I am not so sure I want to. Oh well, brother or not, I am not going to let this bully whip me.

The next two hours, we had classes in geography and history. Those are my favorite subjects, but the time still passed very slowly. I wasn't afraid, but I just couldn't get the fight off my mind. I knew we would get a spanking from the school principal for fighting. That, too, was standard procedure. I also knew that if I got marked up in any way, like getting a black eye or a cut lip, to show that I had been in a fight, I would get a whipping when I got home. That was the whipping I was dreading. My father did not fool around when he gave you a whipping. He used his razor strap, and he always laid right into it.

Each morning, when I would leave for school, my mother would say, "Now don't you get into a fight today. If you do, you will get a whipping from the school principal, and you will get another whipping when you get home. But don't you take three whippings. If you get into a fight at school, you win that fight." I was going to get two whippings for sure. But I was going to win the fight with Tom Dully. Getting into a fight was just too much trouble and I wasn't looking forward to it. I just wanted to get it over with.

At long last the noon bell rang. I did not even take my lunch pail with me when I went into the schoolyard. I didn't want to fight on a full stomach. If you get hit in the stomach right after eating, you might throw up your lunch. There was going to be a lot of people watching and I didn't want that embarrassment.

All of the kids in the school would be watching the fight, but they would not interfere no matter who won. It was my fight and I had to deal with it. Father had trained me well, and I wanted to take advantage of all the training he had given me. I went out in the schoolyard and sat on a wood rail situated in the back of the school building. I knew that was where the fight would take place. I was ready.

A few kids were just hanging around, waiting for the show to start. Tom Dully and his two friends did not show up for several minutes. When they did come around the corner of the school building, a large group of students was right behind them.

Tom walked right up to me and said, "Are you going to just sit there, or are you going to stand up, so I can knock you down?"

I quickly stood up and said, "OK, I am standing up. Now, let's see you knock me down."

He came in with a wide, swinging right, which I ducked and allowed the swing to just pass over my head. Then I came up with a right upper cut, into his breadbasket, which knocked the breath out of him. It didn't knock him down, but it hurt him bad, and I could tell by the expression on his face that it really surprised him.

I just waited for him. Now, I knew that I could beat him.

He came in slow the second time, and in a boxing stance. I could tell by the movement of his feet that the boxing stance was just a pretense at knowing how to box. I still waited with my hands at my sides, waiting for him to make his move.

He made the same mistake again. He came at me with a swinging right. I just moved back out of his reach and let the swing pass, then moved in behind his swinging right, with a stiff left jab to the nose. It caught him solid. He went down hard with a bloody nose. I could tell by the look in his eyes, which were filled with water, that he couldn't see very well.

Then I made a mistake. I reached down to give him a pull up.

I underestimated him. He was not a good boxer, but he was a very determined fighter. He came up with a swinging right again, but this time I was not expecting it, and the blow caught me over the left eye. He followed the right cross with a left hook into my stomach, which made me glad that I had not eaten my lunch.

That event taught me a lesson that I would not forget. Never underestimate an opponent. Now I was going to have a black eye, and I would for sure get a whipping when I got home. That made me mad, but I remembered my father saying, "Never get mad while you are in a fight. Your anger will work against you. It will make you take foolish chances."

So all right. I will just settle down to business. I came back at him in a boxing stance, watching his eyes, waiting for his next mistake. I didn't have to wait long. He made a lunge to grab me. He wanted to take advantage of his size to wrestle me to the ground. I side-stepped him and put my right leg behind him, and my right arm across his chest and neck, and threw him over my hip to the ground, in what was aptly called, a schoolboy throw.

I did not extend my hand to pull him up this time. I just stood over him, waiting for him to get up. When he did, I stepped in with a short left jab to the nose and followed with a hard right uppercut to the chin. He went down again. This time he just sat there. While sitting on the ground, he said, "We will finish this tomorrow."

"Surely you are not crazy enough to try this again, but if you are, I'll be waiting. Any time you are ready."

I walked back into the schoolroom to get my lunch and was sitting eating it, when two boys and a girl came and sat down beside me.

The girl said, "Thank you for whipping him. He has had that coming to him for a long time. He beats up on every new kid that comes to this school. Maybe he will think twice before he picks on someone smaller than him next time."

One of the boys with her was her brother. He put his hand on my shoulder and said, "It was sure good to see him take a licking for a change, but you had better watch out for him. He will try it again, when he feels he has an advantage. He will get his friends to help him get you down; then he will take advantage of his size and hold you down while he beats you."

The girl was looking at me with the nearest thing to admiration I had seen for a long time. It made me feel a lot better. She was dressed in old worn, clothes, as I was. She was not very pretty, but she could be if she had some nice clothes and had her hair done up in curls like the girl in the fifth grade. I asked her what grade she was in. She said she was in the fourth grade, and her name was Martha. I told her, "My name is Danny Duncan."

"Oh, everybody in school knows what your name is," she smiled. "I have to go to my room. Will I see you tomorrow?"

"I will be at school tomorrow. I hope we will see each other."

She smiled and walked away. I was feeling much better now. The two boys walked with me back to class. They were both in my classroom.

When we got back to the classroom, Miss Pringle said to me, "The principal wants to see you in his office." Her voice was not harsh, and her face showed sympathy. She knew I was going to get a whipping for something that was not my fault.

I looked over and saw Rebecca Dully looking at me with a sneer on her face, which said, "Now you will get what is coming to you for beating up on my brother." Surely, she knew the fight was not my idea. It was forced on me by her brother. If she knew, the look on her face sure didn't show it.

When I got to the principal's office, Tom Dully was already there, sitting in a chair in the corner of the room. The principal's name was Mr. Bingham. He was a big man with dark hair and dark, deep-set eyes. He looked a little flabby for a man of the early west. I guessed it was because he spent his days sitting behind a desk, instead of walking behind a plow or working cattle. He did not look like an unkind man. I felt he would be fair.

Mr. Bingham was seated behind his desk. He looked at Tom and me, and said, "All right, you two, stand up here in front of my desk. Now, which one of you started that fight?"

I stepped forward and said, "I did." Mr. Bingham knew, and I knew that he knew, who had started the fight. It was only one of the many fights that Tom Dully had started as the school bully. But I was not going to let Tom off that easy this time. I was not going to let him play the martyr.

Mr. Bingham looked at me in surprise. Tom was quick to see what I was doing. He was a bully, but he was no dummy. He stepped forward and said, "He did not. I started it."

"I hit first," I said.

"Yeah! But I swung first and missed, and then you hit me, so I started it."

I was beginning to like this guy; he had spunk.

Mr. Bingham was suppressing a laugh, and his face showed it. "All right, I've got to give you two a paddling. Who wants to be first?"

We both said, "I do," at the same time.

He took Tom first, and laid ten pretty good licks on him. Tom didn't let out a whimper. I was thinking, *This kid is tough. I hope, some day, we can be friends.*

Mr. Bingham dismissed Tom. I was next. He walloped me ten times also, but I could tell his heart was not in it. I knew I would not be this lucky at home, when my dad took his strap to me.

When Mr. Bingham finished with his paddle, he turned me around and asked, "Are you going to become the school bully now?"

"No sir, I don't like fighting."

"They tell me you do a pretty good job of it. Where did you learn to fight like that?"

"My father taught me."

"I thought so. I would like to meet your father some day."

"I think you would like him, but he sure is going to give me a whipping when I get home with this black eye."

"Fathers have to do what they have to do. Now go back to class and take this note to Mrs. Pringle."

I do not know what was in the note, but she smiled when she read it.

The afternoon classes passed without event, but I found myself wondering about the homely, little girl who had been so kind to me after the fight. I kept remembering her smile.

After school, I stayed to talk to Miss Pringle. I asked her about the story she was reading. I told her, "I would like to read the first part of the story that you are reading to the class—the part I've missed."

She took me to the library and showed me how to check the book out of the library. She said, "You can read it at home and catch up on the story."

I had to hurry home. I must help my brothers milk the cows and tend the animals before supper. Then I would get my whipping, go to bed to read my book, and think about the next day of school. I was wondering if I would see the little girl from the fourth grade. Will I have to fight Tom Dully again?

A brief moment in time
William Wayne Dicksion

The Hawk

At the time of this event, I was 10 years old.

One early, summer day, when my family was living on Spring Creek, a red-tailed hawk was circling in the clear, morning sky. It was waiting for an opportunity to kill another of my mother's chickens.

The hawk was almost as big as an eagle. Either he, or another of his type, had carried off some of our baby pigs and several full-grown chickens.

Mother said, "Son, I am tired of that hawk stealing my hens. Go get the gun and shoot it."

My two older brothers and I used guns often around the farm. We used them for bringing in food for our table, such as rabbits, squirrels, quail, wild geese and ducks in season. We also shot nuisance animals like wolves, rats, and rattle-snakes. We practiced with the guns every chance we got. Any of the three of us would have been considered an expert marksman with rifles. We did not own or use handguns.

The guns we used were small-caliber rifles and small-gauge shotguns. I did not like to use shotguns; they damaged the game too much. So the request that Mother made for me to get a gun and shoot the hawk was not an unusual request, even for a 10-year-old boy who had been using guns as tools on the farm for several years.

Our father taught us how to use a gun and gave us very strict orders on what a gun could and could not be used for. A gun was not a toy. It was a tool, just like an ax or a shovel was a tool.

"OK, Mom. But that hawk is a mighty wily, old bird. I am not sure I will be able to shoot him, but I will see what I can do."

"Take the 22-caliber rifle and put some cartridges made for long range in it. That hawk probably won't let you get close, so you will need the cartridges made for shooting greater distances," Mom said.

"OK, Mom, I'll get him if I can."

I took the 22 rifle from the rack over the back door. I made sure to keep it concealed under my jacket. If the hawk saw the gun, it would be very difficult for me to get close enough to get a good shot at him. Somehow, hawks seemed to recognize and know about guns.

Mother was hanging clothes on the line to dry, and when I walked by, she said, "The last time I saw him, he was flying up the creek. He won't go far. He'll just be waiting until we go inside the house, and then he'll come back and kill another hen."

As I walked around a bend in the creek, I saw him. He was sitting in the top of an old, dead tree, not more than a hundred yards away. I quickly placed the butt of the rifle to my shoulder, hoping to get a shot at him before he got a chance to see me. I wasn't quick enough.

He saw me before I could draw a bead on him. He flew away. He only flew a couple of hundred yards, just far enough to be out of range, and there he landed in another tree. The hawk knew I was after him, and he knew I had a gun. He was going to be very difficult to kill. The only way I was going to get a shot at that old bird was to sneak up on him. I began walking back in the direction from which I had come. I wanted that hawk to think I had given up and was going back to the house. As soon as I got around the bend in the creek, out of his sight, I changed my direction and continued stalking the hawk. This time I walked through the trees growing alongside the creek. I hoped the trees would enable me to stay out of sight of the hawk. Just before I got in range, I did a foolish thing. I accidentally stepped on a dead stick. When that hawk heard the stick snap, off he went! Again he flew just out of range.

That hawk was just playing with me. He was taunting me. I could almost see him grinning. He was beginning to make me mad. How in the world could that hawk know the range of my gun, when I hardly knew it myself, especially with those long-range cartridges in it? The last place the hawk stopped was on a branch in the top of a big cottonwood tree. It was on the boundary of our property. The barbed wire fence, which marked the property line, was nailed to the tree the hawk had landed in. The hawk was not really off our land. I felt it would be all right for me to shoot him. It was eating our chickens and Mother had asked me to shoot it.

The hawk was more than 200 yards away. There was no chance for me to get any closer. It was all open ground between the hawk and me. I was hidden behind some small trees. I knew that if the hawk saw me, it would be long gone. It would take more than an expert shooter to shoot that bird from this distance. It would take a lot of luck also. I placed the barrel of the gun in the fork of a tree to steady it. The slightest movement of the gun barrel would mean a big miss. The hawk was sitting right in the top of the cottonwood tree, in plain sight. I took aim four inches above his head to allow for a drop of the bullet in flight. It was considered bad shooting to shoot an animal in the body. You were supposed to shoot it in the head. I took a long time steadying the gun. The slightest pull while squeezing the trigger would cause the bullet to miss the target. I very carefully squeezed the trigger and the gun fired. For a time nothing happened. Then, to my amazement, the hawk fell from the tree as if he had been hit with an ax. The reason nothing happened right away was I had failed to account for the flight time of the bullet traveling such a distance. I just stood there dumbfounded. Was it possible I had made that shot? I ran to the base of the cottonwood tree to look for the dead bird. I looked and looked. No bird! I knew I had seen him fall! No bird falls like that unless he is dead or badly wounded. At last, I looked across the fence and lying there on the sandy bank of the stream, on our neighbor's property, was my hawk flopping around like a chicken with its neck wrung.

I wanted that hawk! I wanted to prove I had been successful in my effort to kill it. I placed my gun on the ground and crawled through the barbed wire fence to get my hawk. He was wounded, but he was still very much alive. I had only shot him through the neck. I knew that a hawk, especially one of that size, could be very dangerous. I pondered how to pick him up. I decided the best way was to grasp the feathers on his back. That was a mistake. When I picked him up, he twisted around and sank the talons of his right claw into my belly. I grabbed the other foot to prevent him sinking those talons into me, also. The talons of his claw had gone all the way through the flesh of my belly and he was grasping a good-sized chunk of me. I knew I had to kill him or he was going to hurt me badly. His neck was injured so he could not use his beak, thank God. Holding his right talons with my left hand, I picked up a fallen branch and began trying to beat him off me.

While I was struggling with the hawk, the neighbor who owned the property on which I was now standing rode up on his horse. He made no offer to help me. He just sat there and laughed! I felt he should be helping, instead of just laughing. He continued sitting on his horse, just laughing. His inconsiderate behavior made me very angry. We were not raised to tolerate that kind of mistreatment. I threw the heavy chunk of wood I was using on the hawk at him. I hit him and damn near knocked him off his horse. I was so mad, I yanked the hawk off me and the hawk's talons took a big chunk of me with them. I then twisted the hawk's head off, climbed back through the fence, picked up my gun, and took my prize home with me.

When I got home, I was still bleeding a lot from the wound the hawk had inflicted on me. When I walked up to the farmhouse, there was blood running down the front of my right leg. That was one of the only times I ever saw our father show concern for an injury any of us kids had sustained. Dad was a harsh man. Even when we were very young, if we cried, he would say in a very stern voice, "Are you going to grow up and be a man, or are you going to remain a baby all your life?"

In a few minutes, the neighbor rode up on his horse to complain to my father that I was hunting on his land. I had told my parents of the episode at the fence. Father asked the man if the story I had told him was true. The man, in a very arrogant manner, said, "Yes, but the hawk was on my land!"

Dad glared at him and in a very quiet voice, which dripped with ice, said, "If you ride away quickly and never show yourself here again, you might prevent me from pulling you off that horse and beating the shit out of you."

The man turned and rode away, his horse in a full run.

We nailed the hawk's wings to the hay barn door. The span of the wings reached across the door. That was the only animal trophy I ever took in all my life, but I was proud of that one.

A brief moment in time
William Wayne Dicksion

The Quicksand

I was eleven years old. It was summer time. Our older sister had come home for a visit. She was working as a school-teacher and living away in the big city. When she came home, she brought with her the ten-year-old son of a friend of hers. The boy was to stay with us on the farm for a while in the summer.

An extra boy on a farm with a large family of boys was no trouble at all and our sister knew it. Mother would just put a little more in the pot when she cooked our meals. When we slept in the summer time, we slept just about anywhere we happened to be when we got sleepy. Sometimes we would sleep in the hay in the barn or in a stack of hay in a field, and sometimes in the bed of the wagon. Our father said that we slept more like a pile of dogs than like people. For my brothers and me, it was a quick and easy way to sleep; no trouble getting up or down. We liked it that way.

Looking back on those times, to my brothers and me, every day was just another day, but to that boy and the other boys she brought home to the farm, every day was an adventure to them. Those boys are old men today, and I'll bet that those men are still telling their grandchildren of their summer on the farm.

Each morning we would get up, go out to the pasture and get the cows, drive them into the barn, feed and milk them. We would gather the eggs and tend to the other animals. We had horses, mules, cows, pigs, chickens, and sometimes sheep and goats. All of these animals had to be cared for. This city boy knew the difference in the animals, but he had no idea what needed to be done to care for these different animals. He had to learn it all. We had lots of fun watching him trying to learn and kidded him about it. He seemed very dumb to us, but I am sure we would have been just as ignorant trying to learn the things we would need to know to live in his world. Right now, we weren't in his world; he was in ours. He took the kidding well. We sure admired his spunk.

He wanted to learn to milk a cow. We put a bull in a milking stall and told him that was the cow he would learn to milk. You should have seen the look on that bull's face when the boy sat down on a milking stool beside him. We all laughed so hard, even the cows seemed to enjoy the humor. He also saw the humor and took it in good spirits. We all admired him for being so good-natured about the joke we had played on him, so we gave him a gentle cow to start learning how to milk. After a few days, he was able to milk the cows, and was a big help with the milking.

The next big learning experience for him was even more humiliating. It was an event involving quicksand on the creek. Quicksand is not at all what it has been depicted in the movies. There was a lot of quicksand along Winter Creek in those days. When we were kids, we liked to play in it. It is not dangerous to people who understand what it is and how it works. Quicksand is nothing but particles of sand held in suspension in quiet water. The particles of sand are so thick in the water that it can look just like regular sand. The top of the sand can dry, giving it the appearance of dry sand. If you don't know what to look for, you can be fooled by it and never suspect that it is there, until you find yourself down in it. When the surface tension of the water is broken, all of the sand held in suspension will quickly drop to the bottom of the water.

If you accidentally stepped into quicksand, and did not recognize what you had done, you could sink to the bottom, just as though you had stepped into water. Quicksand is at least as dense as water. If you just lay over on your stomach, you will float on it, and you can just slither out like a snake. If you do not know that trick, you could be in serious trouble, if the quicksand is deep and you do not get out of it quickly before it settles around you. The danger of quicksand is, if you do not get out of it quickly, the sand will settle, and you are trapped. It can settle so tightly that unless you know what to do, you could get caught in it and drown.

Sunday afternoons was a time when we could play on the creek. All of the creeks had names. Some of the other creeks we had lived on were Walnut Creek, Bitter Creek, Spring Creek, and Haystack Creek. The rivers they ran into were Washita, North Canadian, South Canadian, Arkansas, Cimarron, and Red River.

The name of the creek we lived near at the time of this event was Winter Creek. The area which it drained was sandy soil. The creek did not run through a canyon. It had a flat alluvial plain, and flooded often when the heavy spring rains came. The streambed was sandy. That is why there was so much quicksand. The sand filtered the water, leaving it clean and clear. At the bends of the creek, holes would wash out, leaving nice, clean, clear ponds, which were wonderful for swimming or fishing.

Our favorite swimming hole was a place where the creek ran across a ledge of white limestone, leaving a small waterfall. The water going over the falls dug out a hole in the sand, leaving a very nice pond of water. The pond was about twenty-feet wide and about forty to fifty-feet long; a wonderful swimming hole. Most of the kids growing up along those creeks learned to swim there.

On this particular Sunday afternoon, a group of us was going for a swim. The group consisted of my older brothers, Dave, the boy spending the summer with us, and myself. We spent the summer wearing only the smallest amount of clothing we had to wear. I guess the only thing that kept us from going naked was our mother's strict religious upbringing. I always felt sorry for the girls. They had to remain covered from head to toe. I thought there must be something bad about a woman's anatomy for them to need to keep it so secret.

We were all barefooted. The sun had tanned us until we were the color of copper pennies, after they got tarnished. The swimming hole was about a mile from our farmhouse. We were all strung out in a line, following the cow trails which always led to a watering place for the animals. We were running, walking, laughing, talking, and gathering wild sand hill plums as we went along. By the time we got to the swimming hole, we were all a little too warm and ready for the nice, cool water. We all shed our clothes while we were taking the last few steps to the pond and in we went. Some diving, some jumping, some just splashing in. We frolicked in that pond of water for about two hours. Soon we had to go home to milk the cows and do the farm chores. We were reluctant to get out of the water.

There was a spot of quicksand which existed just outside of the swimming hole area in which we loved to play. It was not deep. We would only sink in up to our armpits and then we would be standing on the limestone ledge which formed the waterfall. We liked to wait until the sand would settle tightly around us and then we, knowing how, would work the water back into the sand so we could slither out like a snake. We knew how, but our visiting companion did not. Not a word was passed between us, just a look and a nod and we all knew what we were going to do. We waited until the sand settled completely around Dave. It was as though he was encased in concrete. We very quietly crawled out of the sand, not saying a word about how we were getting out. The sand had settled so tightly around Dave that you couldn't have gotten him out with a jackhammer.

My brothers and I worked our way out of the sand, jumped into the nice clean water of the swimming hole, washed ourselves off, and got dressed, just talking away about everything except Dave's problem. My oldest brother was our leader. He called out to Dave to get out of the quick-sand and get dressed.

He said, "Dave, let's go. We have to go milk the cows."

Dave had seen us get out with what must have seemed to him to be no trouble. He struggled and pulled against the sand, but to no avail. He was stuck. He was a plucky kid and growing up as we had, we admired his courage.

He didn't call out to tell us of his trouble. He just continued to pull against what had been quicksand, but was now nothing but solid, packed sand. We pretended not to notice his plight. Since we were fully dressed, which meant we had our shorts on, we started walking off down the creek as though we were going back to the farmhouse. We had walked about fifty yards, when we heard this plaintive call.

"Hey! I seem to be caught!"

I will never forget the sound of that call. We all began laughing. We were laughing so hard, we could hardly stand. Poor Dave now realized he had been the butt of a joke.

He was standing there, encased in sand up to his armpits, helpless as a kitten. We walked back to him, laughing. He appeared chagrined. We knew exactly how to get him out. We had done it many times, getting animals out of just such a trap. We gathered around him, tromping our feet up and down, working the water back into the sand like patting the water back to the surface of a mud cake, or a patty cake as we called it. We slid him out, washed him off, and started home. He could have done the same thing for himself, if he had worked his hands up and down to work the water back into the sand. But without that knowledge, if he had been alone, he would have been there for the duration. On the way back to the farm, after he had gotten over his embarrassment and saw the humor of the situation, he joined us in a good laugh.

The summer passed, the autumn came, and Dave went back to his way of life in the city. We never saw or heard from him again after that summer. I have often wondered whatever happened to him. He had the qualities needed to become a good man, and I'll bet he turned out to be one hell of a man.

A brief moment in time
William Wayne Dicksion

The Lesson

We were living on Winter Creek. Our farm was located approximately seven miles north of a small farming community with a population of maybe a hundred people. It contained the usual businesses of all small, farming towns–a grain terminal, a cotton gin, a farm implement store, and a repair service. And, of course, it had a general store and a grocery store. For the women, it had a clothing store and for the men, it had a pool hall. For the children, it had a park and a playground with a baseball and softball diamond. It had a high school with a basketball court, and one or two family-style eating places, where hamburger and milkshakes were the most common foods served. The hamburgers were made with the highest quality of meat and the milkshakes with the best ice creams and milk. The farmers knew the difference and demanded the very best. There was always a movie theater for the families and it was a place where the high school kids could go to on dates.

The town was located in the valley of the Washita River. Spring flooding was so common that most of the building in the flood zone were built up on piles with elevated wood sidewalks. They were built up about two feet off the ground with plenty of room under them for the dogs, cats and the town drunks to sleep under.

The town had a one-armed constable who carried a long-barreled, revolving pistol. He was tough as a boot heel. He was a likeable guy until a firm hand was required. Then he could and did deal with the problem with whatever degree of force was required.

It had been raining for days, and all of us boys were itching to go to town, shoot some pool, and go to the movie. It didn't matter what was showing at the movie. It was always a single feature, and we would sit through it again in case we missed something the first time. Then we'd go to the Bon Ton Cafe to get a grilled cheese sandwich and a strawberry milkshake, maybe even a piece of pecan pie.

The creeks and the Washita River were all flooding. Dad did not want us to ride the horses into town for fear we would hurt the animals by having them swim across the river. The only thing left to do was to swim the flooded creeks and river, and walk the seven miles to town. Dad was not concerned about our ability to swim the flooded streams; he knew that crossing those streams would present no difficulty for us teen-aged boys.

We would simply find a floating log, all hold onto it and kick our way across the stream, then walk on to the next stream and do it again. Of course, we had to take off our clothes each time. We did not wear shoes, so that presented no problem. We knew that we were going to look a mess by the time we got into town. The merchants didn't mind. We were customers at a time when there were only a few people making their way into town. Our biggest concern was crossing the river. The flooding was not high enough to flood the town, but it was high enough to make it too dangerous to try to cross the bridge. The valley was flooded both sides of the bridge anyway. The log we chose for floating across the river was good, maybe a little too good. It carried us more than a mile downstream, and we had a difficult time making our way back to the road which led into town.

We went straight to the pool hall. The pool hall was strictly a place for men. We were not men yet, but we did men's work and we were accepted without question. Farmers and ranchers were sitting around tables, playing dominos. They played a game of 21and gambled small amounts. The game was more for recreation than for gambling. The young men all liked to shoot pool. The more skilled players would play snooker and make small wagers. We were not that good. It cost five cents per player to play. With two players at each of the tables, the house made ten cents per game. There were about six tables in the place, so the proprietor did pretty well.

There were two men playing at another table near us. They got into an argument about their game. They had both been drinking. They got louder and louder. The owner of the pool hall came over and tried to quiet them down. He was having no luck. It became obvious that a fight was about to begin. The owner called for the one-armed constable. He came right away and tried to quiet them down and settle the dispute between them. They started giving the constable a bad time. With only one arm, he could not keep them both under control. He pulled out his pistol and banged one of them over the head, dragged him out, and rolled him under the elevated sidewalk. Then he took the other one to the jail. The jukebox in the pool hall was playing the song, "I'm walking the floor over you." The people of the town were walking back and forth on the elevated sidewalk, over the man lying under it. I was standing in the street watching this and laughing my head off. When the constable came back for his second prisoner, he, too, saw the humor of the situation and joined me in a good laugh.

For about 50 cents each, we could have a big night on the town. When we worked for hire, we could make about ten cents per hour. Fifty cents was a lot of money. At ten cents per hour, it would take five hours of labor to earn 50 cents. Fifty cents then would be the equivalent to about forty dollars today. We could play three games of pool for fifteen cents, go to the movie for a dime, go to the cafe and have a hamburger and a milkshake for five cents each, and have money left over for a big little book.

A big little book was the forerunner of the comic book. It had the same kind of cartoon drawings as the comic books of today. It was called a big little book because it was four inches wide, four inches long, and nearly four inches thick. In some of them, the cartoon characters were drawn in such a way that when you turned the pages fast, the characters would seem to move.

By the time we had completed our big night on the town, it was about 10 o'clock. We are supposed to be home by midnight. There was no possibility that we could make it.

We were going to catch hell when we got home, but there was nothing we could do about it now. So we started the long trek home. It was not raining, but there was still a heavy overcast of storm clouds, no moon, no stars. The night was blacker than the inside of your hat. That presented a real problem when we had to swim across the flooded streams. Should one of us get into trouble, he had to be able to call out to let the others know of his plight. There was safety in numbers. It was so dark; we had to remain close together to stay in contact.

The Washita River was the biggest stream we had to cross. We walked about three-quarters of a mile upstream so the moving water would carry us down to what we hoped would be near the road on the other side. It worked! We crawled out of the river just upstream from the road. So far, so good, but we still had six miles to go and more streams to cross. It was getting late, and we were getting tired. No one was saying a word, just plodding along in silence. Mile after mile we walked, stream after stream we crossed. Finally, we came crawling out on the north bank of Winter Creek. The farmhouse was only three-quarters of a mile farther. We could see a glow in the eastern sky where the sun was coming up. The sun was rising clear, indicating that the storm had passed. Any other time it would have been a beautiful sight, but we were just too tired to care.

As we were walking across the porch, heading for our beds, we heard our father's voice saying, "It's too late to go to bed. The cows have got to be milked."

Them damn cows! Again I vowed to one day find a better way to make a living than by pulling the tits of a bunch of cows.

There was no need to grumble. The only way out of this situation was to go milk the cows. After the milking was done, the milk must be processed. The other animals had to be fed, the barn cleaned and made ready for the evening milking. By the time we completed the morning chores, Mother had breakfast ready. We were really too tired to eat. I could hardly wait to get to that bed.

We started for the beds when Dad said, "Come on boys, we've got to cut wood today. We've got to get ready for the winter."

It is Sunday. It is June. We never worked on Sunday other than tending the animals. The creek was flooded; we couldn't even get to the damn trees to cut wood. I knew what was happening. No one had said one cross word about how late we had gotten in. This cutting of the wood was the scolding I was expecting.

There was a big stand of willows near a spring on the hillside, about a mile from the farmhouse. Dad said, "This is the wood we will cut for firewood, for the coming winter."

It was summertime. The day was going to be hot and humid. Willow wood is the sorriest wood possible for burning in the stove or fireplace. Had the old man flipped his lid? No, he hadn't flipped his lid. He knew exactly what he was doing. We worked all day cutting that sorry wood.

When the sun finally went down, Dad said, "OK, boys, we had better go milk the cows." I was thinking I would like to shoot every damn cow on the farm! About 10 o'clock that evening, we had the animals all tended, the cows milked, the milk taken care of, and finally we ate supper. By this time, I am wondering if I can make the walk to the bed. I don't even remember my head hitting the pillow.

That was the most effective disciplinary action I ever experienced, and a lesson I will never forget.

A brief moment in time
William W. Dicksion

The Sunrise

The year is 1938. The world economy is still in a terrible condition. In the central portion of the United States, there is a great drought in progress. The area is referred to as the dust bowl. So many farmers are being forced to leave their farms that some small towns are becoming ghost towns.

I am the fourth child of a farm family with nine children. We have no money to buy even the necessities of life; our family is struggling to survive and we are in danger of losing our farm. There are hundreds of men looking for work. There is no work to be had in the entire area.

It is early summer and school is out. I must do what I can to help provide for our family. My mother and father are reluctant to have me leave the farm and travel seeking employment, but there is just no other way.

I left the family farm three days ago, and I am looking for a place where I can work to earn money. It is my hope that I will be able to send enough money home to help my father make the payments on the farm and prevent the bank from foreclosing. The farm is all we have; it would be devastating for the family to lose it.

I am 13 years old, and I am walking along old Highway 66 somewhere in West Texas. The land is flat, and the day is warm. In the distance, I can see the horizon, shimmering from the heat rising from the land. I have to keep wiping the perspiration from my brow to keep it from running into my eyes. My ride ran out down the road a mile or two where I started walking. It didn't make any sense to just stand and wait for a ride. The highway goes on and on and one place is as good as another to catch a ride. It doesn't matter where the ride is going as long as it is going west. That is the way I am going, west.

Looking down the road, I can see an old pickup truck coming. It is still a half a mile or more away. I watch it coming. As it gets closer, I can see it is not so old; it is just hard-used, like many farm or ranch trucks are. I can tell by the weather-beaten, old felt hat the driver is wearing that a rancher or farmer is driving the truck and that the driver will not be going far, just to his ranch or farm or to whatever town is nearby where he goes to get supplies. I am just standing, watching as he approaches. He sees me while he is still a hundred yards or so from where I am standing. He starts to slow down as he looks me over. After he passes me, I can tell by the way the truck is slowing that he is applying the brakes; he has decided to give me a ride.

I walk up beside the truck. The driver opens the door on the passenger side near me and says, "Hop in, Son, where are you going?"

His manner is straightforward and his voice is friendly. The driver is a man about fifty years old with weather-beaten hands and face. His clothes are typical ranch clothing; a plaid shirt, denim pants, and heavy, leather belt and riding boots. His smile is open and I know this is a man I can trust. I step up into the truck and in answer to his question, I reply, "West." He gives a little chuckle and says that would be California. I laugh and say, "Yeah, I guess you're right. I am following the sun. When I have gone as far as I can go on land, I will probably be in California."

He asks, "What are you doing way out here in the middle of nowhere?"

I tell him that my last ride was with a rancher who turned off the highway to his place back down the road apiece, and that left me out in the country near where he picked me up. He nods and we ride while he tells me that he had been born and raised on the ranch he now owns. Other than the time he spent in the Army, he had lived on his ranch all of his life.

He says, "I like what I am doing and feel no need to go looking for another way."

I tell him why I am traveling. I don't have to tell him why I am hitchhiking; he knows it's because I have no money to pay for bus or train fare.

As we are traveling along, driving through broken country, there are canyons and ravines where the exposed dirt is the color of rusting iron. In the distance, we can see cliffs with higher levels of plateaus and buttes. On the plateaus, I can see timber growing. The faces of the cliffs are of many layers of different colors, such as grey, red, and nearly black.

After riding along for a few hours, we come to a small, crossroad town with the highway on one side and a railroad on the other. We stop at a service station, which has a short-order café behind it. The café serves hot sandwiches and milkshakes. I am a little hungry but I only have a dime. I think I had better hang onto that dime. I might need it down the road a ways.

After filling the fuel tank, the driver of the pickup says, "Perhaps you might want to get off here. I am only going a couple of miles farther, and then I will have to turn off the highway to my place, and you will be left walking along the road out in the country again."

I thank him and tell him that if it were all right with him, I would just ride along as far as he was going.

"Hop in," he says.

When we get to his turn off, there is a dirt road leading away from the main highway, which I can see continuing across the prairie to the right. He stops to let me out and asks me if I am sure that I am going to be all right.

"Oh yeah, I've been all right for quite a while," I reply.

He laughs and says, "You'll do just fine. I'd bet my hat on it."

This time, I wait beside the road, watching the cars passing. I can tell by the way the cars are loaded, that the people in the cars are people moving west. They are not tourist or vacationers. These are serious-faced people with a deep purpose in mind. Like me, they are seeking a place to live and work. They are seeking a new way of life.

Many have mattresses on top of their cars. These mattresses are their beds at night. Like me, they are sleeping beside the road. They camp beside the road, cook their food, sit beside the fire while talking, and then go to sleep on the mattresses. Probably one of the people traveling in the car would stay awake at night, to keep watch while the others slept. They have no money for motels or hotels. They are worried about having enough money to buy gasoline for their old cars, so that they can reach their destinations.

I am watching, and I am a part of, a great migration west.

After about an hour of waiting for a ride, the sun is setting. It looks like a giant ball of fire slowly sliding down behind the distant mountain range. I wait beside the road until about a half hour after sunset. I watch the colors fading from the sky. It is beginning to get dark. I know that there is very little chance of getting a ride at night. I walk out on the prairie to find a place to sleep before it gets too dark for me to see my surroundings. I find a suitable spot with good grass for a cushion and not too many rocks to lie on, or for vermin to crawl from under.

While I am looking for a place to lie down for the night, I find a few wild onions and sit there chewing on them as I watch the darkness closing in. I am watching and listening while the whole world settles down for the night. In the immediate area, the land is flat with a few gullies eroded here and there. There are cacti and mesquite growing on the prairie, with an occasional willow or cottonwood growing along the gullies where enough moisture has collected.

In the distance to the west, I can see the foothills of the Rockies. I know I will be entering them soon, and I am looking forward to that with great anticipation. I have never seen the mountains and it will be a great adventure for me. The sunset glow is fading fast. The first light to go is the light near the eastern horizon. The last light to go is the sunlight reflecting off the high, thin clouds in the western sky. I hear cattle lowing in the distance. Then I hear the lonesome call of a couple of coyotes off somewhere in the night. I can feel the day coming to an end. Everything is becoming quiet.

There is a stillness settling around me. All I can see are a few fuzzy shadows of objects near by, as darkness gathers. I take an extra shirt from my duffle bag and put it on to ward off the night chill that I am sure will be coming as the coolness of the night air replaces the warmth rising from the ground. When all of the reflected light is gone from the high clouds, all is black except the stars in the canopy of sky, which reaches from horizon to horizon. There is no artificial light to be seen anywhere. The darkness is complete, and the stars are displayed in all their splendor. I am fascinated by the three-dimensional array of lights against an ink-black sky.

Using my bag for a pillow, I lay there on my back looking up at the stars and thinking, *This must be what it was like for all humankind before there were so many people to distract them from the beauty around them.* To me, it was almost an ethereal experience, watching the night all alone with no sounds except the sounds I made. I can hear myself breathing and hear my heart beating. I feel I am one with the whole universe. I must have watched for more than an hour. I don't remember falling asleep.

I awake. I have no idea how much time has passed. I have no watch and even if I had one, it is too dark for me to see. I had grown up on a farm, and I had slept outside many times, but never quite like this. I am all alone in a completely strange environment. I know no one, and no one knows me. The only possessions I have are a dime in my pocket, the clothes on my back, and the clothes I am using for a pillow. That is it. I don't even know for sure where I am. I know that I am somewhere in the semi-arid desert of eastern New Mexico. While riding with the rancher, we had crossed the Texas/New Mexico border. I lay there wondering how long until morning. I am thinking about what lies ahead of me.

I know that I must have something to eat soon, and I have only a dime. I am no thief, and I am sure not going to beg. I know how to get food from the prairie—I can trap a rabbit or a quail. I know how to clean and cook them, but that will take too much time. I have to find work to enable me to earn enough money to buy food.

I feel, more than see, a slight yielding of the darkness in the east. No, it is just my imagination. I hear a rustling in the grass to my right; there is something else, besides me, awake. I wonder what it might be. A snake? Nah, a snake makes no sound as it moves unless it is being chased; there is nothing to chase a snake, so it is not a snake. It is too early for a ground squirrel; probably just a field mouse. Yeah, it's just a mouse. Whatever it is, it is not bothering me and I have no reason to bother it.

I look again to the east. It *is* getting lighter. I see a faint horizon. The stars are not as bright as they were. In a little while, I can see a trace of light in the sky. I see a horizon….The trace of light is becoming a white glow, very faint, but a glow. Time passes. The fuzzy shadows around me are beginning to take shape.

Soon there is a little pink, mixed in the white on the horizon. The world is stirring, like a child, rubbing the sleep from its eyes. I watched the world go to sleep last night, and now I am watching it awake. The white on the horizon has now turned to red and gold. There is a faint wisp of clouds reflecting the growing light. I can hear the cows again. I feel and hear them moving in the distance, probably going for their early morning drink of water. The little, wild animals that live on the prairie; the prairie dogs, the ground squirrels, the chipmunks, the quail, and the meadowlark, are all stirring. I hear a calf call out to its mother, and the mother moos her reply. There is a slight movement of the air, a breeze, ever so light. I feel it like a caress on my cheek. The silhouettes are now identifiable, the landscape is showing color, and I can see the green in the trees. The whole world seems to be holding its breath as the sun breaks. A crescendo of light streams across the sky, lighting everything around me.

A new day is born, and I am a part of it. I feel that I have helped the night give birth to the day.

Now I have to make a decision. I have traveled more than a thousand miles in three days. I am getting tired. I am hungry, and I need a bath. Do I continue hitch hiking west and hope to find work to pay for my meals, or do I go back to the little crossroad-town where we had stopped the previous evening? I figure there are four opportunities for work at that little crossroads. There is the service station, the granary, the restaurant, and the farmers stopping in for service. The people who operate any one of those things might be willing to hire me part-time. At the service station, I could pump gas, fix tires, and do lube jobs. I could work at the granary. I have had a lot of experience moving grain around. Some of the farmers or ranchers might need help, and I have done most all of that kind of farm or ranch work.

I decide my best bet is to walk back to the little town. I know what is there. To continue west is to take a chance. I have not eaten for two days, and I'm hungry. I walk the two or so miles back to the little town.

I walk into the café, sit down on a stool at the counter, and order a cup of coffee and a doughnut. The price of a cup of coffee is 5 cents and a donut is 5 cents–there goes my dime. I want a chance to size the place up. I need a job. There is a man working the place alone. He is doing the cooking, waiting the counter and the six tables that make up the restaurant, washing the dishes, keeping the place clean, and working the cash register. He is a very busy man. I don't know if he can afford help, but he sure needs it.

I say to him as he comes by, "Looks to me like you need a dishwasher."

He looks quizzically at me and sizes me up in an instant. "I sure do," he replies. "Can you wash dishes?"

"I am the best dishwasher you will ever see."

"When can you start?"

"Right now."

He hands me a dishcloth and says, "There is the sink."

With no further exchange, I start washing the dishes and cleaning the counter and the tables. We close the place at 6:00 P.M. Then we sit and talk for a bit. He says he will pay me two dollars per day and all I can eat. That "all I can eat" part sounds very good to me. I say, "I'll have a hamburger and a milkshake." He smiles and makes them for me. I tell him the pay will be just fine, and I will see him tomorrow morning.

In the back of the restaurant, there is a makeshift shower and an old sink with some soap lying on the wooden frame. I use them to take a bath and wash my hair. Then I wash my clothes. I have everything I need. In the days that follow, I wash my clothes after work, take the wet clothes with me to where I sleep, and hang them on the shrubs after dark, knowing they will be dry in the morning. I take them down from where they are hanging, fold them, and put them in my duffel bag before daylight.

After the first night, I walk out on the prairie, find a better place to camp, and make myself a better place to sleep. I gather some grass to make a bed under a ledge of rock that water has eroded in one of the gullies. The ledge of rock provides a little protection should it rain. Also, I will be able to build a fire should I need one. I never do build one. I do not want to disclose my place of residence.

I sleep much better. I have had something to eat, a bath, food in my stomach, a better bed, clean clothes to wear, and a job to go to. I am in seventh heaven!

The next morning I go to the café at 5:30 and wash myself in the sink which is located in back of the restaurant. Then I open the café, start coffee, and wipe down all the tables and the counter. The place is ready for customers when the owner arrives. He is very pleased and fixes my breakfast first thing. I meet many interesting people. Most of our customers are people who stop for fuel at the service station. They are travelers going east or west on Highway 66.

Farmers and ranchers who live nearby stop in from time to time. I get to know some of them. They are curious about me. I am a stranger in their midst. When they ask me where I live, I tell them, "Oh, just outside of town." The expression "just outside of town," when you are talking about the Great Plains, could be two minutes, or ten miles.

Once a woman asked me if my mother knew where I was, and I told her, "No, but she has lots of other kids to worry about." I don't think the answer satisfied her, but she was polite enough not to pursue it further. The customers who interest me the most are the families moving west. They are mostly very poor, and they eat sparingly. Some of them have the gaunt faces of people suffering from malnutrition. I want to help them by giving them food, but I have an employer to be loyal to.

Two weeks pass and I decide to draw my pay. After I am paid, I will have money in my pockets, and I feel it is time for me to move on. I tell my employer that I have to continue west and ask him to pay me for the time I have worked. He says he is sorry to see me leave and will give me a raise if I will stay. I tell him, "No, there is something waiting for me out there, and I must go on to find out what it is." He asks me to write and tell him if I ever find what it is that is waiting for me. He says, he too, had looked for it at one time. He says he had been unable to find it, so he finally gave up and stopped looking. But he asks me to let him know if ever find it. If I find it, perhaps it might give him the courage to try again. I tell him that I will let him know. He pays me 28 dollars from the cash tray. I pick up my duffle bag, walk out on Highway 66, and continue west.

In California, I did find better paying work. I worked at the shipyards in San Pedro for the remainder of the summer, and returned home with enough money to help my father make the payments on the farm.

A brief moment in time
William Wayne Dicksion

The Flood and the War

In the winter of 1940, we moved to the farm on Winter Creek. It was a beautiful farm with fertile creek-bottom land. Our father anticipated some good crops. At last, he had some good land. He plowed the fields, and planted corn and cotton. The seeds sprouted and he had some beautiful fields.

Then the rain came. Rain is good for farmers, but it rained and rained. The water in Winter Creek began to rise. The rain continued, harder and harder. Soon the water in the creek began to overflow the banks. The water ran across the newly planted fields. The flooding increased until all the fields were covered with the floodwater. All the crops were ruined.

There was nothing to do but wait for the land to dry and replant the crops. Before the fields could be replanted, the land had to be made ready again. The erosion from the flood had washed gullies across the land. Those had to be filled before he could prepare the land for planting. The good soil was now covered with sand and silt. It was discouraging, hard, time-consuming work. Replanting the fields was a big expense for Dad. He had to purchase all new seeds and he never had much money; I am sure Dad had to borrow money to replant. Having to replant would make the crops mature late. The crops would not be as good, and the prices he could get from the corn and cotton would be less. But there was no choice but to replant. To miss a crop totally would be devastating.

Finally, the fields were replanted. The new plants were looking pretty good, not as good as before, because the soil had been damaged, but at least there would be a crop and some income from the land. To labor for a full year and receive no financial reward for your labor is terrible.

Again the rains came. The fields flooded. Again, the crops were ruined. It was too late to replant. Another year's labor was lost. Dad was disappointed, despondent, and angry. He became hard to get along with. The only emotion a man is allowed to show is anger. There was more than the usual quarreling between Mother and Dad. Our home was an unhappy place. Going to school was a respite, but it was only temporary.

Our only source of food was from our garden, which was on high ground and the flood did not destroy it. We got food from our animals. We could get milk, butter, eggs, and meat. From the garden, we got vegetables. From the creek, we caught fish and picked wild fruit. We had no money, but we did not go hungry. With no crops to harvest you would think there would be less work. Not so. The land must be prepared for next year's planting, and now the silt and sand were covering the soil even deeper. There was wood to be cut for heating our home and for cooking. The animals must be tended with even greater care. We worked for other farmers to obtain enough money for some of the things we had to have.

The following year was a repeat of the last. Again, after the crops were planted, the rains came. There was flooding and devastation. The flooding continued. There were five floods one after the other, destroying the crops and the land. Our father was economically devastated. He had borrowed money on his farm and on his cattle, to rebuild his land, and replant his crops. No crops, no income, and no way to pay the loans. There was nothing left to do but sell the farm, the cattle, and the farming tools to pay the loans.

So, on a cold winter day in December of 1941, we held an auction and sold the farm and everything we owned, even the furniture in the house. To lose the farm was bad, but to have to sell the animals was even worse. They had become almost like members of the family—especially the horses. That was a sad, sad day.

I was given the task of providing hot coffee for the people who attended the sale. Mother had a big black iron kettle, which she used to heat the water for washing clothes. It would hold about twenty gallons of water. I filled that kettle with water, built a fire under it, and brought the water to a boil. I don't know where I got the coffee, but I dumped an entire can of coffee into that boiling water. Then I reduced the fire to just coals to keep the coffee simmering. The coffee grounds settled to the bottom of the pot and we had some of the best coffee anyone had ever tasted.

Everyone was talking about the bombing of Pearl Harbor. No one knew where Pearl Harbor was or why anyone would want to bomb it. All the young men were talking about joining the military to fight the "Japs." No one had ever seen a person of Japanese ancestry, but everyone knew that they were very bad people. They were responsible for the bombing.

I never knew how much we sold the farm for, but we must have ended with a little extra money, because Dad bought a farm in western Oklahoma and we moved there in the dead of winter. The farm was located on the plains. It was bitter cold; the wind came howling across the flat land. The house was very small, our family was large, and there were only limited amounts of wood for heating. We had no money, no animals, no garden, and even the creek was just a miserable little ditch with bitter gray water. For the first time in my life I knew real hunger.

We lived off the land, much as the Indians had done before the white man came to the area. We gathered wild fruit, nuts, and berries. We caught the fish from the little streams, and hunted the wild birds and rabbits. In this way, we had some meat for the table. Because the family worked together to do the things that were necessary to survive, we made it through the winter.

My father, my two older brothers, and I worked at whatever we could find to make extra money. At long last, the spring came. We bought a couple of milk cows and some chickens. We were on our way to recovering financially. After two years, we bought a bigger and better farm.

It is now 1942. The depression has passed. World War II is raging in Europe and in the Pacific. My older sister is away somewhere teaching college. My oldest brother has enlisted in the Army Air Corps and is a crewmember on a B-17. His letters said he was flying missions over North Africa. Another brother, who is two years older than I, has been drafted into the Army and is in training at a base in California, awaiting shipment to Europe.

I am now 17 years old. I have spent much of the last five years away from home working to earn money to send home to help the family survive the great depression. With my two older brothers and sister gone, I was needed at home to take the lead in doing the work on the farm. I completed my last year of high school before I enlisted in the Air Force. I wanted to be a fighter pilot.

There was a place at Altus, Oklahoma where a person could enlist in the Air Force. I enlisted and passed the examination for flight training. I was thrilled. The enlistment occurred at a time when many young men were being called up for the draft. My enlistment was to become effective when I was called for the draft.

When the time came for me to report for the draft, I was not required to undergo the physical examination since I had already been accepted by the Air Force. I was not informed of this, so I underwent the regular physical examination.

The summer before, while working in the wheat harvest in Oklahoma, I was exposed to excessive wheat dust, which left scar tissue on my lungs. The X-Rays revealed those scars and I was classified as unfit for military service. When the

Air Force was informed of my condition, they also rejected my enlistment.

That was by far the most devastating thing to happen to me in my entire life. The path my life would take was forever altered on that fateful day. I was rejected, dejected, and humiliated. Everything changed in one moment. Now I must find a new direction, and a new purpose. I left Oklahoma in deep humiliation and went to California. When I arrived in California, I went to work in a defense plant and started college.

A brief moment in time
William W. Dicksion

Hitchhiking

The shimmering heat was rising off the blacktop highway, leaving the illusion of water standing on the surface of the road. As I walked toward the illusion, it would move away from me, ultimately disappearing altogether, leaving only the searing, hot surface of the paved road. I realized how it could drive a person mad who was starving for water.

In the silent loneliness of the prairie, I could hear the cars coming before I could see them. When I looked back to see the approaching car, it would appear to be an aberration or another illusion as it approached through the heat waves rising off the road. As I watched it coming, I would try to determine if there might be an opportunity for a ride with this vehicle. I had learned, after hitchhiking for a few hundred miles, that there were certain factors which would increase or diminish my opportunity to get a ride. If I were to get a ride, and there was only one occupant in the car, that person would have to be a man. If there were two persons, the *driver* would have to be a man; the passenger could be a man or woman, adult or child. If there were three persons in the car, the chances were slim that they would stop to give me a lift. If there were four or more persons in the car, they for sure would not stop.

I was fascinated by the whining sound the tires would make as they rolled on the hot, paved surface when the cars passed. I wondered, *What is the cause of the strange sound?* I knew it was because of the tread of the tires rolling on the paved surface, but there was more to it than that—some of the tires were nearly bare and still they caused the sound.

I played a game of trying to figure out where the cars and their occupants had come from, and where they might be going. If they were not going to give me a ride, the adults in the car would never look at me as they passed. The children, if there were any in the car, usually would look at me and sometimes wave to me. I never felt bad, or even disappointed if they did not stop. I knew that they, too, had their journey to make and it just did not include me. Eventually, there always would be someone who would stop.

Some of the lone drivers would stop because they just wanted someone to talk to. Having someone to talk to helped them stay awake on their long drive to whatever their destination. Some would ask me if I could drive. They were looking for someone who could help them drive, so they could take a break from the tiring task of long hours of driving alone. Some stopped just because they wanted to help someone who needed a ride. That would usually happen when there was a man driving and the woman with him was of a motherly type.

I learned to read the faces of the people. Some were kind. Some were lonely. Some were just curious. Some had hidden agendas. I learned to spot those quite easily and I would find a reason to decline their offer of a ride. I felt sorry for them;

they were the sad ones whom I could see needed help more than I did, but I was in no position to help them with their problems. Usually, the help they needed was far beyond my ability to provide.

Hitchhiking gave me a wonderful opportunity to learn to take the measure of people. Those lessons served me well as I made my journey through the tangled roads of my life.

I had no real destination. I was simply going west. Wherever west was, and whatever was there when I arrived, was enough. If I caught a ride, I was lucky and rode it as far as it went. When the ride ended, I simply caught another ride. If I did not catch a ride, I made do with whatever the situation provided. My only needs were food, water, and a place to sleep. A place to sleep was no problem. To me the whole southwest was a place to sleep. I grew up in the country, and I was raised close to the earth. I knew how to deal with the creeping and crawling things that I might encounter in spending a night sleeping on the ground out in the open. In fact, I liked it. I liked the silence. When there were sounds, they were usually distant and muted.

I liked the game of identifying the sounds. Most of them were very familiar to me. The yipping sounds of the coyote, the lowing of cattle, the sounds of the little creature scurrying in the grass and brush. On rare occasions, I would see a scorpion or a snake. I had a working agreement with them—if they didn't bother me, I would not bother them. They always kept their part of the bargain, and I kept mine.

There is an amazing amount of food in the wilds of the southwest. The Indians lived on it full time; I surely could live on it for a few days.

I would camp near a stream if I could find one. It would provide water for me to drink, food for me to eat, and a place to clean myself up. If there were no stream, there usually would be a pond that the farmers or ranchers provided for their animals. Most of those ponds contained small fish, crawdads, and bullfrogs; all of which could provide me with food, if the need arrived. I knew how to catch them. I knew how to clean them and I knew how to cook them. I had no problems that I could not overcome.

When the rains would come, I could always find shelter beneath a bush, a bluff, or a rock. I liked the rain. I liked the smell of the rain on the dry soil. It cleaned the air, and after the rain, it was as though the world had been reborn. The little animals would come out to enjoy the freshness of the newly cleansed world. The leaves and the flowers of the plants would stand up and shine with a new glow; they too were pleased. After the rains had passed, I would continue my journey. With each mile, I would see a new place, meet a new person, and experience a new adventure. I learned that difficulties and troubles were merely things to be overcome.

A brief moment in time
William Wayne Dicksion

Catching Fish

We were poor and when we went fishing we were not fishing for fun or sport, we were fishing for food. Here are a couple of methods we used to catch fish.

When the flow of the creeks would subside, there would be ponds of water in the creek with just a trickle of water between them. The ponds would be four to eight feet deep, about 10 feet wide, and 20 to 30 feet long. Some ponds would have quite a few fish in them and, of course, there would be fish of all sizes in the ponds. Some of the fish were big enough to eat and some were too small. Naturally, we were interested in only the larger fish. When we would try to catch the fish on a fishing line, the small fish would keep getting the bait off our hooks and we would spend a lot of time trying to catch the ones that were large enough. We devised two methods that worked very well for getting only the fish we wanted.

By using shovels, we would build small earthen dams across the stream to stop the flow of water long enough for us to use one of the two methods we had devised to harvest the fish we wanted.

One method was to gather green walnuts from the trees, place them in a burlap bag and beat the bag of green walnuts with a stick until the sap from the hulls of the nuts would seep out. We would then drag the bag back and forth in the water, and the sap from the green hulls of the nuts would make the fish sick. When the fish got sick they would float to the top of the water. We'd gather just the fish we wanted with a net and put them in a smaller pond of fresh water until they recovered from the stunning effect of the toxins in the sap of the green walnut hulls. After we had gathered the fish we wanted, we would break the earthen dams and allow the fresh water of the stream to flow back into the pond. The fresh water would revive the rest of the fish and they would continue to populate the creek with fish for harvest later. It was an old Indian trick and it worked like a charm.

Another method we used, which was a little more work, but it was an even better method of getting just the fish we wanted. This method was to dam the stream above and below the pond. Two of us would stand with our backs downstream and each of us, by using scoop shovels like oars, would throw the water out of the pond. The water we threw out would continue to flow downstream. This method was so efficient that two persons working steadily could throw about 300 gallons of water per minute down the stream and could empty a pond in no time. The fish was then easy to pick up from the bottom of the creek. We would gather just the ones we wanted and then, by opening the dam above the pond, allow the pond to refill. If there were more fish than we needed to eat at that time, we would place the fish we did not need in the lakes on the farm. The fish would help control the mosquito population in the lakes and we had a source of fresh fish to use at another time. This method was better than a refrigerator because the fish in the lake would continue to grow larger and provide more and more food.

You would get into a lot of trouble doing that today. I don't recommend you use either of these methods for catching fish.

A brief moment in time
William Wayne Dicksion

Coyote Run

It is late summer of 1942. We have harvested our wheat and I am plowing the land, getting it ready for replanting. The fall semester of school will be starting soon, and I am in a hurry to get the plowing done.

The morning is half gone and I have plowed a strip of land 200 yards wide. There is an outcropping of rocks near the middle of the field, which is covered with grass, weeds, and small bushes. It is a haven for small game such as rabbits, quail, and other animals. They use it for nesting in spring, shelter from the heat in the summer, and protection from cold in the winter. The rocky area covers about an acre of ground.

In the distance, I hear the baying of hounds and I know that the hunt club is chasing a coyote. The men ride horses following the hounds as they do in the fox hunts in England. I can tell by the baying of the hounds that the run will be coming near me. I begin looking for the coyote they are chasing, and I see a young female coyote running across the plowed land. She is running toward the outcropping of rock. I hope she will not try to hide in the rocks because the hounds will have her trapped. The land is plowed all around the rocky area, and it is too small for her to escape into. To my dismay, she runs along side and makes a leap into the rocks. Then to my surprise, out jumps a young male coyote. He is bigger and stronger than the female. He is fresh and fast! The female remains hidden in the rocks and the male takes her place in the run. I can hardly believe what I have just seen. Are animals really that smart? I stop my tractor to watch as the hounds and riders go by. Sure enough, the hounds take up the trail of the new coyote. I sit on my plow, watching the chase with a big smile on my face, as the hunters fade into the distance chasing the fresh coyote. The young female remains securely hidden in the rocks.

About an hour passes. I hear the hounds again. They are following the same route as before. The male coyote comes into view running across the plowed land toward the rocky outcropping. He is following almost the same path the young female had taken earlier. I am wondering, are they going to do it again? Sure as sunrise, he runs alongside the rocks, makes a big leap into the rocks, and out jumps the female! I am so astonished by what I have seen that I stop my plowing. I have to watch this! The hounds are farther behind this time and I can tell by the way they are running that they are exhausted. The hounds run past and continue after the now refreshed young female.

One by one the riders come to where I am sitting. They stop their horses to rest and talk. Both they and their horses are exhausted. One of the riders, whom I knew well, asked, "Have you seen a coyote?"

"No," I lie. "I have been busy plowing and haven't seen a thing." There is no way that I am going to reveal the coyotes' secret. That is the cleverest thing I have ever seen animals do.

The lead rider says to the others, "We may as well call off the dogs; there is no use running them to death. That is the runningest coyote I have ever seen." One of the riders blows on a bullhorn and the hounds stop baying and walk back to the riders. The leader of the riders asks, "Will it be all right if we leave our horses in your corral to rest them?"

"Yeah, that will be all right. There is water in the tank and hay in the loft."

They ride away toward the barn looking beat. I am pleased by how the run has turned out. I have never approved of their method of killing coyotes. I do not approve of killing animals, just for the fun of killing.

I continue my plowing, thinking, *I will never again underestimate the intelligence of an animal. If a general had devised strategy for battle that had worked that well, he would have been called a military genius.* We think of animals as having cunning, but we do not believe they have the power to reason. Perhaps we are wrong about that.

As I finish my plowing, I am wondering, *Will the two coyotes get back together?* That evening, after sunset, I hear the mournful call of a coyote, and in the distance I hear a reply. I learn a lesson that day, and my life has been enriched.

A brief moment in time
William Wayne Dicksion

Lost in the Snow

The time is January, in the winter of 1943. We are living in Western Oklahoma. The landscape is flat and barren. There was a comment some people made to describe the land. They said, "The only thing between Western Oklahoma and the North Pole is a barbed wire fence, and it is down in most places." The statement is well made. In winter, when the north-wind blows and it gets cold, it gets very cold.

The day began as a normal day—gray, dusty sky, with a light wind blowing from the northwest. As the day progressed, a dark cloud appeared on the northern horizon. Everything got quiet. There was a feeling of impending danger in the air.

Dad said, "Son, you had better saddle a horse and bring in the cows. Put them in the corral and put out some hay for them. It's going to get cold and we can't afford to lose any animals."

The cattle were scattered across a wide area of the flat pastureland. I saddled Ol' Brownie. He was getting old; he was developing some arthritis in his ankles. He didn't like to be ridden because most riders expect too much out of him and it hurts his ankles to jump ditches or make fast starts and fast stops. He knew I would never ask him to do foolish things like that so he liked me to ride him. I shared my candy with him when I had any. We were buddies. He was a smart, gentle animal and he could be depended on not to cause trouble in a pinch. He was my choice of a horse to ride. I knew this rounding up of the cattle was going to be difficult and time consuming. I was working alone; I didn't want a skittish horse under me if things went bad and I had to deal with a contrary cow or steer.

The storm hit before I could get the cattle all bunched together for the drive to the corral. The wind was howling out of the north. Heavy driving snow was falling. The swirling snow made it difficult to keep track of all of the cows. I could identify on sight each and every animal we owned. However, I didn't want to depend on my memory, so I counted the animals I had rounded up. We had thirty-seven cows in that pasture, and I counted thirty-seven animals in the gather, so I started them to the corral.

The pasture land was north of the barn and corral; the wind was from behind us. That should have made the drive easier, but the wind-driven snow was beginning to drift. The cattle began to wander trying to find shelter from the storm. Working by myself made it necessary to chase after each animal to keep the drive all together and it was difficult to keep track of just how many cows I had in my herd. It was taking more time than it should under normal circumstances. It was getting late in the afternoon before I got the herd to the barn.

Dad had the corral gate open, and he had already put hay in the feeding troughs. That helped a lot to get the cows to go through the gate and into the pen. I rode Ol' Brownie into the shelter of the barn and was feeling pretty good. I could unsaddle my horse and go inside where it was warm. I was looking forward to having a good, hot cup of coffee and getting my feet and hands warm.

Dad was counting the cows as he always did. He walked into the barn with a worried look on his face and said, "Son, you missed one. It is that old brindle cow that is missing. She is a contrary animal and probably wandered off in the storm. You have to go get her. She will freeze to death in a storm like this. Did you have her in the herd when you started them to the barn?"

"I don't remember her specifically but I started in with thirty-seven head."

"Well, looks like she just wandered off somewhere along the way; she shouldn't be too hard to find. You had better go get her. She will freeze to death for sure."

I pulled the ear flaps of my winter cap down over my cold ears, put cloth gloves on under my leather gloves, patted Ol' Brownie on the neck and said, "Well, ol' buddy, we gotta go back into the storm to get one more, so let's go." He moved his head up and down as though he understood. We moved out of the shelter of the barn and into the teeth of the storm. The temperature on the thermometer on the side of the barn showed ten degrees below zero. The wind was blowing up to fifty miles per hour. I estimated the wind chill to be around forty below.

As I was leaving, Dad called out, "Now don't you get lost out there. We would never find you in this storm."

I yelled to be heard over the sound of the wind and told him, "I know every inch of that prairie. I'll be OK."

Dad nodded, and I rode away on Ol' Brownie. I didn't have a watch so I didn't know for sure what time it was, or how long I had been searching, but I could tell it was getting dark.

The snow was coming down harder and harder. The drifts were getting deeper and covering all of the landmarks. The swirling snow was making it difficult to maintain my sense of direction. I knew the wind was coming out of the north so that helped some.

I had been riding for a long time and I hadn't seen hide or hair of that damn cow. Because of the swirling wind and the driving snow, I could see no more than twenty feet in any direction. It was getting darker and darker.

I finally realized I wasn't sure just where I was. I could find nothing that I recognized that would give me a clue as to the direction I should ride to get back to the barn. I didn't want to go back without that cow, but I had lost all feeling in my hands and feet. I couldn't feel the reins in my hands. I had to keep looking to make sure I had not dropped the reins. I had lost all feeling in my ears long ago. I found myself wondering if my ears were frozen and if I should brush my gloved hands against them, would they break off? *I gotta get back before Ol' Brownie and I both freeze to death, but which way should I go?*

I dismounted and removed the saddle. I was hoping the warmth of the horse would help me to keep warm. I threw the saddle under a mesquite tree, wrapped the saddle blanket around my shoulders, and with more than a little difficulty, remounted the horse.

For the first and only time in my life I was lost. I knew that horses have a built-in sense of direction, so I patted Ol' Brownie on the neck and said to him, "Let's go home." His head bobbed up and down, I loosened the reins, and sat huddled up in the saddle blanket. Ol' Brownie started walking briskly in a direction I thought was wrong, but I wasn't going to interfere. I sure didn't know the way, and all I could do was hope Ol' Brownie did.

I have no way of knowing how much time passed before, in a frozen stupor, I saw the shadowy outline of the barn, looming up out of the darkness. Ol' Brownie didn't stop until he was inside the barn.

I was so cold I couldn't dismount. Dad and one of my younger brothers came and helped me off the horse. I would have fallen for sure if I had not had help.

I took Ol' Brownie's head in my arms and said, "Thank you, ol' buddy. I couldn't have made it without you."

Dad said, "The old brindle cow wandered in about a half hour after you left. We were getting worried about you, and were about ready to come hunting for you."

A brief moment in time
William Wayne Dicksion

The Well

We were living on a farm in western Oklahoma. The water was contaminated with gypsum. Our only source of potable water was rainwater, which fell on the roof. We caught the rainwater in gutters and drained it into a cistern.

Dad felt that it might be possible to dig a well and get potable water. He told J.D. and me that he would pay us one dollar a foot for digging a well. J.D. and I jumped at the chance. We figured we could dig at least four feet of well per hour, and we could make a lot of money. The going wage for farm work was 15 cents per hour.

We began digging right away. The first six feet of digging was easy and we were making money. As the hole got deeper, it became more difficult to get the dirt out of the hole. It wasn't too hard until the hole was about ten feet deep. Then we had to make a windless to draw the dirt from the well with a bucket. Using only one bucket to remove the dirt was too slow, so we rigged a method for using two buckets. By using the two-bucket method, we could lower one buckets into the well on a separate rope, pull the full bucket up with the windless, while the empty bucket was being filled. It worked well, but it was very tiring. We alternated work posi-ions and that helped. The hole kept getting deeper and the work kept getting harder. At 36 feet, our moneymaking came to a complete stop. We hit a ledge of granite rock. We needed to know the thickness of the rock. We borrowed a rock drill from a neighbor, and by using a sledge hammer and the drill we pounded a hole in the rock.

We made the hole about 18 inches deep. We reached the limit of our drill and there was no end of rock in sight. Now what do we do? J.D. said he had seen dynamite used and he thought we could blast the rock with dynamite. We drove into town and bought six sticks of dynamite, two blasting caps and ten feet of fuse. The man selling the blasting material told us that the fuse was very slow burning, and asked if we knew what we were doing. We told him that we were old hands at blasting. I could see the doubt in his eyes, but he sold us the stuff anyway.

We returned to the well, and filled the hole with dynamite in preparation for blasting. The only way to get out of the well was by climbing the rope. J.D. and I got into a serious discussion about who would go into the well to light the fuse. I decided that J.D. would light the fuse.

J.D. said, "You know I can't climb a rope worth a damn."

I did know that, and I told him that I would pull him up with the windless. He seemed doubtful, but he finally agreed to descend into the well to light the fuse.

Before he went into the well, we decided to test the fuse. We cut a four-inch length of fuse, lit it, and timed it to see how long it would take to burn. We calculated that it would take ten minutes for two feet of fuse to burn. That would be plenty of time to climb out of the well, and move to a safe distance before the charge would go off.

We thought it best to give ourselves a little extra margin of safety, so we cut the fuse a few inches longer than the two feet. J.D. climbed into the well, hollered up to me, "Are you ready?"

"Yeah, I'm ready."

He lit the fuse and I have never seen a monkey climb a rope faster than he climbed the rope out of that well!

We ran about 50 yards upon a hill to wait for the blast. We forgot to check our watches for timing the fuse, and decided to just wait until it went off. We waited. We waited. And we waited. It seemed like a very long time.

J.D. said, "I think the fuse has gone out."

"No, let's wait a little longer."

We waited. Still no blast. After a while, we both decided that maybe we should check to see if the fuse had gone out.

We crawled on our bellies down to the well, approaching the opening with caution. Just as we were ready to stick our heads out over the hole to see the fuse, KERWHAM! The dynamite went off. The earth shook. Dirt and rock came out of that hole like shot out of a shotgun. After a while, all was quiet. Then rocks began falling. We put our arms over our heads in an attempt to shield ourselves from the falling rocks. Some of those rocks would have weighed 50 pounds. They were lethal projectiles. To say that I was scared would be the understatement of the age. All went quite. We just lay there wondering what might be coming next. After a while, we decided it would be safe to look into the hole.

The blast had blown an additional six feet of hole into the bottom of the well. The ledge of rock we were digging into was about two feet thick. There was a crack between two layers of rock. The blast had gone into the second layer of rock four feet, leaving the bottom of the hole round and smooth as a pot. Between the two layers of rock there was a stream of water that was cold and clear. A beautiful well!

We took our father to see the well. He looked at it and tasted the water that we had drawn. He shook his head and said, "Well, boys, that is a damn good well. It's a shame the water is no good."

The water was laced with gypsum. It was unfit for man or beast.

The only thing left to do was to fill the hole so that nothing would fall into it.

Digging the well was hard work, but we learned a lot.

A brief moment in time
William Wayne Dicksion

Trip to California

In May of 1943, I completed my 11th grade at the Eastview High School. World War II was raging in Europe and Asia. My two older brothers were away fighting in the war. We rarely heard from either of them. Naoma, my oldest sister, was living away somewhere. We had moved to a farm west of Eastview High School. It was bigger and better than the previous farm. The land was better and easier to work.

I had four dollars I had earned working for a neighboring farmer. Farm wages were very poor. Fifteen cents per hour was considered good wages. I decided to work during the summer in California.

I stuffed a few clothes in a Navy-type duffle bag and started down the road. I was heading west. It was a long walk to the paved highway, seven miles of dirt road. I hoped I might have a chance to hitch a ride. If I got lucky, a farmer might come by and offer me a ride. It was a long way to California. I had no money for motels. I knew I have to spend the night wherever my ride ran out and night overtook me. I had an extra shirt and a light jacket in my bag that I could sleep in if it got cold. I had the bag for a pillow and the entire Great Plains to lie down in, what else would I need.

It took me more than two hours to reach the highway. I continued walking in the direction I wanted to go. I had walked for about half an hour when a pickup truck pulling a trailer stopped to offer me a ride. As I got into the truck, I noticed that the driver had a horse in the trailer with its head tied down. I thought, *That is a strange thing to do.* As we rode along, the driver said he was a retired businessman from Chicago who had bought a ranch in West Texas and was going to be a rancher during his retirement years. I instantly knew that I was talking to a real green horn. In the first place, ranching is no retirement—it is very hard work. No man in his right mind who knew anything about horses would haul a horse in a trailer with the horse's head tied down. A horse is naturally nervous in a trailer and is not going to like the ride when he can't see where he is going. The horse was kicking the end and sides of the trailer. I was afraid that the horse was going to hurt himself, so I said to the man, if you will let that horse get his head up, he will ride better.

The man looked at me quizzically and asked, "Do you know about horses?" I told him that I had worked with horses on our farm. He then asked me if I would do what was necessary for the horse if he stopped the truck.

I got into the trailer with the horse. There was a closed container with water in it. I gave the horse a drink, gentled him a bit, and loosened the rope so he could get his head up. I got back in the truck and said, "We can go now; the horse will tolerate riding in the trailer much better now."

The owner was impressed and asked me if I would train the horse for him. I told him that I was on my way to California but I would give it a few days, enough to gentle the horse so that he would be able to ride him.

We continued to the ranch, which was located in southwest Texas. He had bought about a section of land. That was not considered a good-sized farm in West Texas and it sure was not a ranch, but to this Chicago businessman it must have looked like a very big parcel of land. The man's wife was already at the ranch house. She welcomed me into their home and I spent the next few days working with the horse. I had agreed to gentle the horse enough for someone to ride him. That was different from breaking a horse to ride.

The horse had worn a halter and lead rope before, but it had never had a bridle on. My first problem was to train the horse to wear a bridle. He was a young horse. I guessed that he was no more than two or three years old. The horse, being young, was an advantage to me. He probably had never been hurt and was not afraid of people. I got a bridle on him after a little struggle. I spent the next couple of hours just petting him and leading him around with the reins. Then I put a saddle blanket on his back and continued to just gentle and pet him. Every few minutes I would offer him feed and water. I would take the blanket off him, rub him down, and put the blanket back on him. Then I brought the saddle out from the tack room, laid it on the ground in the corral, and let him smell it and get used to it. After an hour or so, I picked up the saddle and placed it on his back. He did not know what to make of the saddle, but it didn't frighten him. I led him around for the rest of the day.

The owner was watching me and asked, "Why don't you just get on the horse and ride him?"

"This is not Hollywood," I said. "This is the real thing. I don't want to break the horse; I want to train the horse."

He said no more.

The next day, I went through the same thing, just gentling the horse, petting, feeding and watering him, putting the saddle on and taking it off, and letting him walk around with the saddle and bridle on. The owner's neighbor watched me work the horse. He never said a word; he just watched. But I could tell by his actions that he was a seasoned rancher with a lot of experience with horses. I also could tell he had never seen a horse trained this way before.

On the fourth day, I asked the neighbor if I could use his plowed field to train the horse. I told him that I would re-plow it for him after I was through using it. He looked puzzled and said that it would be all right. I led the horse around in the plowed field for a while. I knew that if the horse were going to buck, the plowed field would tire him quicker, hurt his hooves less, and if I fell off, I would get hurt less by falling on soft, plowed ground. The rancher was watching all this, but he still did not say a word. I continued petting the horse, and then very gently stepped up on his back. The horse turned his head around and looked at me but he didn't pitch. I just sat there on his back petting him. After a few minutes, I got off and led him around some more. Then I led him back to the barn, took everything off, fed him, and turned him out to pasture.

On the fifth day, I called him and he came into the corral all on his own. The horse walked right up to me to be petted. I put the bridle and saddle on him with no problem, led him into the plowed field, and got on him. I leaned forward in the saddle and urged the horse to walk forward. I spent the rest of the day training the horse to respond to the reins, to move forward and to turn when I wanted him to.

The following day, I asked the owner to work with me, to allow the horse to get used to him. I instructed him to pet the horse, lead him around, feed and water him, to get acquainted, and make the horse his. He wanted to get on the horse. I told him no, not yet, but to spend a lot of time with the horse.

On the seventh day, I told him to get up in the saddle and pet the horse. Then I told him, "Now urge the horse forward with the reins."

Within a couple of hours, they were a pair. The new rancher rode the horse all around his place. Both he and the horse were enjoying the experience. He came back with a big smile on his face.

The neighbor watched all of this. He walked up to me with his hand extended and said, "That is the damdest thing I have ever seen." He asked, "Where did you learn to do that?"

I replied, "I learned to do that by falling off a horse onto hard ground."

He laughed so hard he was holding his sides.

The horse turned out to be quite a good saddle horse. The owner was pleased and asked me to stay and work for him. I thanked him and said no, my destination was California.

He asked me, "What is this thing with you Okis and California?"

I replied, "California is as far west as we can hitchhike."

We had a good laugh. He paid me 20 dollars, gave me a ride to the highway, and I continued west.

After walking for only a short time on old Highway 66, I caught a ride with a family who lived just west of a small town in New Mexico. They were a nice family and the man even offered to buy my dinner, but I declined. I had lots of money now. I still had the four dollars I had left home with, and the 20 dollars I had been paid for training the horse.

The next ride I caught turned out to be the only ride I ever got which I wished I had not been so lucky. Two men in a new 1942 Chevrolet sedan stopped to give me a ride. It was late in the afternoon and I would normally have waited until morning to continue west but the ride came right away and they said they were going to California. I thought that fate had smiled on me this time. So I settled back. I had the back seat all to myself, my transportation assured all the way to California. I knew that California was a very big place. I didn't even ask where in California they were going. I didn't care. California was California to me and that was good enough.

They continued to drive on through the night. First one would drive for a few hours, and then the other would drive. I thought they might ask me to drive, but they did not. They had the radio tuned in to the police station. I thought it odd, but it did not concern me. I thought nothing about it until I heard on the police radio that they were looking for two men who had stolen a new 1942 Chevrolet. I pretended not to hear the radio. The police were not looking for three men in a car—they were looking for two men in a car. I didn't know what time it was, but it was late at night. We were driving through some very rough terrain. The road had many twists and turns. We saw the headlights of a car behind us and the man in the passenger seat of our car told the driver to "lose them."

He began driving faster and faster. The road was winding and narrow. The car behind us just kept coming. We were screaming around the curving mountain road. I was getting concerned. The man on the passenger side said, "Well, they have a faster car. There is no need to kill ourselves so we may as well slow down."

We had just begun to slow down when a blonde woman in a Buick convertible went by us like we were standing still. I commented, "I don't know where she is going but she must be late in getting there."

We all heaved a sigh of relief. The rest of the night was uneventful, but I sure didn't sleep.

The next morning we stopped for gasoline in a small town along the highway. They now knew that I knew that they were driving a stolen car. I didn't dare get caught out on the desert alone with these two men. I felt there was a good chance I would never make it to California. There was a restaurant right across the street from the service station with quite a few people stirring around near the restaurant. I thought, *This is my chance to be rid of them.* I started across the street to the restaurant.

One of the men stuck his hand in his pocket as though he had a gun and said, "No, you don't; you are with us."

I didn't say a word. I just kept on walking. I was hoping that he would not shoot me with so many people around. The hair was standing up on the back of my neck. I was about half way across the road, expecting to hear a shot. I wondered, *If he shoots me, will I hear the shot?* Nothing happened. I went into the restaurant and ordered a cup of coffee. For the first time in my life I didn't want anything to eat.

The next ride was with a couple on their way to Salt Lake City, Utah. It was out of my way but I decided to ride with them to Las Vegas, Nevada. They let me off on Fremont Street near the Golden Nugget Casino. I had breakfast at a restaurant nearby and paid for it with a five-dollar bill. My breakfast had cost less than a dollar and they gave me four silver dollars in change. I walked into the casino to look around. I watched a dice game. The stick man slid the dice to me. I knew nothing about gambling. But I had heard that 7 and 11 were winning numbers, so I placed a silver dollar on number 7. The table man nodded to the stick man and said, "Take the bet."

I rolled the dice and rolled a 7. I picked up my winnings from that wager, left my silver dollar on the table, and rolled the dice again. I rolled a 7. Again I picked up my winnings and left my bet on the table. There was a man standing at the table beside me. He started to ride with me on my wager.

rolled 7 four times in a row, each time pulling my winnings. The player beside me was letting his winnings ride. I thought I had better not wear out the 7 so I changed my bet to number 11. The table man said, "Take the bet." I rolled 11 three times in a row, each time pulling my winnings. The man riding with me on my bets had a huge pile of chips in front of him. I learned a little about the game by this time, so I moved my bet to the pass line. I rolled four straight passes and picked up my money.

The table man said, "You can't quit now, you're still rolling."

I told him, "I don't want to bet any more."

The man riding with me on my bets said, "Don't go, I will pay you to just keep rolling."

He had won a lot of money. I had been picking up my winnings each time, so I had not won as much, but to me I had a fortune.

I told him, "No, I'm on my way to California."

I picked up my winnings, threw the dice on the table, and walked out. I looked at the table as I walked away. I had rolled a 7. All the players at the table were just shaking their heads.

I had so many silver dollars in my pockets that the weight of the money was about to pull my pants off. I changed the silver to paper, walked a short distance to the bus station, and bought a ticket to Los Angeles.

I will never forget the ride across the desert, then down into the Los Angeles basin. I was seeing trees and plants like

I had never seen before. I was descending into an unknown world.

When I arrived at the Los Angeles bus station, I had no idea how to get from there to my destination of Bell Flower, where my mother's younger brother and his wife lived. I thought that maybe my uncle could give me some advice on how to get a job and get started.

I asked around and was told that I would need to take the PE (that was what they called the Pacific Electric commuter trains). I rode the PE to Bell Flower, and then still had to ask directions about how to get to my uncle's home. I had traveled 1500 miles and was having trouble getting to the last few blocks. After walking for about half an hour, I arrived at their address and knocked on their door. They had no idea that I was coming. They welcomed me with open arms, gave me food, and put me to bed. I slept for a long time. I didn't realize that I was so tired.

I stayed with my aunt and uncle for a couple of weeks and worked for the Triangle Grain Company. My aunt and uncle were good to me and helped me in many ways. I feel I owe them a lot. I did not wish to be a bother to them, so I moved to Long Beach and went to work at the Craig Shipyards.

The Craig Shipyards repaired Navy ships, which had been damaged in the war or just needed repair. It was different from anything I had ever done before. Help was badly needed and they would let me work as many hours as I could. I worked 16 hours per day six days per week. I was being paid 87 cents per hour. I was getting rich.

I found myself a place to live. It was once a big old home which had been converted into an apartment house. It was old, looked bad, and smelled worse. I later found out that the bad odor was because it was so close to the docks. But it was just fine for me as it was within walking distance to where I worked. I was there only to sleep and prepare my meals. I had dry cereal for breakfast, and made sandwiches from luncheon meat to eat at work. One meal a day I would eat at a little fast-food restaurant.

Most of my time was spent either working or sleeping. It was easy to save my money. I had only two problems. They were both big ones, but I could deal with them to complete my purpose; which was to earn enough money to get me through my senior year of high school, and help my family back in Oklahoma.

My biggest problem was contending with drunken sailors who were on shore leave while their vessels were being repaired. To the young service men in those days, the worst thing a man could be was a Draft Dodger or a Zoot Suitor. The nearest I can come to describing a Zoot Suitor is that he was a wildly overdressed young man who was perceived to be avoiding his duty to his country. I was a young man not in uniform, so to a drunken sailor I had to be one or the other—a Draft Dodger or a Zoot Suitor—and it was their duty to beat me up. Since I got off work at midnight, and the sailors were returning to their ships at the docks, there was just no way to avoid them. They were always in groups of two or more. I had to fight my way home every night. The training in self defense Dad had given me and my brothers came in handy. I tell people, "I fought the battle of Long Beach Boulevard."

My second problem was almost as bad. The shipyard where I worked was a Union Shop. That means that you had to belong to the Union to work there. I felt that there were so many men fighting for our country that it was my duty to do the best I could, and the Union did not do that, in my opinion. My way of expressing my disapproval was to wear the Union button on the seat of my pants. The Union Steward wanted the boss to fire me. The boss told him that since I was a good worker and I was complying with the Union rule of wearing the Union button, he had no grounds on which to fire me. I kept my job but it sure caused me lots of trouble, until one day the Union Steward was involved in a labor accident. I was nearby and was able to save his life. Things went a little better for me after that.

It was now September and time for me to return to Oklahoma to complete my senior year of school. I quit my job, took all of my accumulated pay checks to the bank and asked the teller to give the money to me in 100 dollar bills. The amount came to a little more than 400 dollars. The money was easier to carry that way and it looked more impressive. I wanted to show Dad that I <u>was</u> worth my salt. He had always told me, "Son, you will never be worth your salt." Four hundred dollars in 1943 would buy a lot of salt.

My aunt and uncle took me to the bus station in Long Beach, California to catch the bus to Oklahoma. When we arrived at the bus station, I went to the counter to purchase my ticket. While I was standing there buying my ticket, young lady walked up and stood at the counter beside me. She was waiting to buy her and her younger sister's tickets to Noblesville, Indiana. I did not notice that she had set her suitcase right down behind me. When I turned to walk away from the counter, I tripped over her suitcase. I stumbled and fell the full length of the bus station. Everyone in the station laughed. I was not hurt, but I sure was embarrassed and angry. I walked back to the counter where she was still buying her ticket and asked her why she had done such a stupid thing as setting her suitcase right down behind me. I expected some degree of apology, but instead her reply was, "Me, stupid? Why don't you watch where you are going?" This brought on more peels of laughter from the people in the bus station. I did not like her actions but I did admire her spunk, so I joined in with the laughter. I did see the humor of the situation.

When you purchased a ticket, the bus company would allow you to select the seat you desired. I selected the window seat in the first row on the right side of the bus by the front door. I wanted to be able to see out the front as well as have a view to the side. I was first on the bus. I got on and took my seat. Then here came the young lady, who was the source of my embarrassment, and her sister. Wouldn't you know it, they selected the two seats right behind me. I thought, *This is going to be a long ride.* I had to admit they were kinda pretty. With the luck I had with girls, I felt I had better just steer clear. No such luck, the younger one was looking right at me and laughing as they entered the bus. I returned kind of a sick smile and slid down in my seat.

I had been right about one thing; it was a long ride. The bus would make a rest stop every two hours, and a meal stop every four hours. The trip to Dallas took about three days. The seat beside me was empty. At first the girls would occasionally take turns sitting in the seat beside me, and we would talk. Then, as the trip wore on, the older one would spend more and more time with me. I enjoyed her company, and she seemed to enjoy mine. She told me something of her life and I must have told her my whole life story.

The two girls had been visiting their older sister who lived in Glendale. Their sister's husband had been in the Navy and stationed at Pearl Harbor on December 7, 1941. They were returning home for the fall semester of school, the same as I, only they were going to Indiana and I was going to Oklahoma. Needless to say, after spending three days sharing the same seats and every meal for three days we became well acquainted. I had to change to another bus in Dallas while their bus proceeded on to Indiana. Before we parted, we exchanged addresses and promised to write.

The following Christmas I sent the older of the two sisters a Christmas card. I received nothing in return. I never really knew if she had gotten the card. Then one day in late February, I saw a card lying on the dresser in Mother and Dad's room. It was addressed to Bill Dicksion. It was from Noblesville, Indiana. I knew instantly who it was from and why I had not been told of its arrival.

In Oklahoma, everyone referred to me by my middle name, Wayne. My father and I have the same first name. He at times, had been called Bill. I picked up the envelope and removed the card. It was a Valentine from the older of the two girls in Indiana. The only writing I remember was the signature. I laid the card back on the dresser and went to the barn to do the chores. Dad was in the barn working with the animals. When Dad was in the Army in World War I, he had spent some time in Indiana. He had no way of knowing who the card was from. I had never mentioned my meeting the two girls from Indiana.

Very casually I asked, "Dad, who is the person in Indiana that sent you a Valentine card?"

He quickly looked at me and replied, "You know, I have no idea who that is from."

I never said a word. I never told him of my knowledge of the sender of the card. He must have wondered who that card was from for the rest of his life.

There was no further exchange between the girl in Indiana and me, until we again met in California. There must have been some other exchange, but I don't remember when or how I knew she was back in Glendale. I got the information somehow because we resumed our relationship after I returned to California in 1944. We were married in 1945.

Some of the events along the way
William Wayne Dicksion

A Tribute to the True Heroes of the American Frontier

A Day in the Life of a Woman in the Early West

The clock on the wall strikes four. Almeda awakens. Arising slowly, not to disturb her sleeping husband, she removes her homemade dress from a peg and pulls it over her head. She runs a curved comb through her long black hair, pinning it into place. Walking on bare feet, she crosses the floor on rough-hewn, uneven boards that have been worn smooth. While making her way to the kitchen, she checks on her children. The three boys are sleeping like a pile of puppies, huddled together under the warm comforters. Her daughter, in her own small bed with the covers pulled up around her chin, sleeps soundly. She feels her way through the dark house to the kitchen. She lights the kerosene lamp on the table. The lamp needs cleaning; it gives off only a feeble light. She pours water from the pail into a pan and washes her face and hands. She uses no makeup—no powder, no rouge, and no lipstick. Being attractive is not her concern. She has more important things on her mind. Almeda is not a big woman. She is strong and capable. Her eyes are dark and intense. Her nature is kind and gentle, but she can be stern if the need arises.

The three-room house has walls that are covered by coarse blue paper, attached with short nails driven through thin metal washers leaving a buttoned look. The paper serves the purpose of covering the cracks between the ill-fitting boards, keeping out the cold wind in the winter, and the insects in the summer. The blue paper, fading in places, leaves white streaks running up and down the walls. There are three oval-shaped tintype pictures hanging on the wall. Near the backdoor, there is a line of wooden pegs for hanging hats, caps, coats, and jackets. The location of the pegs makes it handy for grabbing what you need on your way out.

The kitchen also serves as a dining room and living room. The room is about 20-feet square. A large oval-shaped dining table seats eight persons. It is the best piece of furniture in the house and the most used. Six cane-bottomed chairs are used for the duel purpose of dining chairs and living room furniture. The strands of cane in some of the chairs are broken, which poke and scratch the person sitting in them. Almeda has placed thin pillows over the worst of them. Sitting on one of the chairs, she pulls on a pair of coarsely made shoes.

A wood-burning stove for heating the house sits in one corner. The pipe for exhausting smoke extends through the roof. The stove for cooking is on the other side of the room near the back door. There is a window over the cook stove allowing the one cooking to view the backyard, the well, and the fields beyond.

Almeda goes to the cook stove to build a fire with kindling that was prepared last night. Using paper from an old catalog, she crumples and places it in the stove, pours a few drops of kerosene, and ignites it with a match. The light from the match seems bright in the dark room. She lays heavier pieces of wood on the burning kindling and soon has a fire hot enough for cooking breakfast.

She picks up a three-gallon pail as she steps out the back door and walks along a footpath to the well. The darkness is less intense outside. It is a crisp spring morning. The sky is filled with stars. She has no time for looking at stars; her mind is filled with the things she must do. This day, like all others, she has more to do than she can possibly get done.

A water bucket attached to a rope and pulley hangs from a crossbeam over the well. Almeda places the pail on the ground and lowers the water bucket into the well. She can tell when the container hits water because the rope on the pulley goes slack. When the bucket sinks into the water, the rope becomes tense again. She draws the water by pulling the rope hand over hand. The water is heavy but her arms and hands have been work hardened, and pulling the rope is no problem. After only a moment of pulling, the container reaches the top. She pours the contents of the bucket into the pail. The glow of the coming morning light glistens in the clear water. Placing the bucket back into the well, she ties and secures it with the rope.

Almeda picks up her pail, carries it into the house, and pours a portion into an iron compartment that has been built onto the side of the stove. The water in the compartment will be heated while she cooks breakfast and used for washing dishes. She also pours water into a fire-blacked coffee pot, puts coffee grounds into the water, and sets it on the stove.

It is time to wake up the rest of the family. She goes to awaken her husband. Gently shaking his shoulder, she says, "Madden, it is time to milk the cows and do the morning chores. You and the boys had better get started. The kids have to go to school today." She goes to her daughter's bed and says, "Get up, Naoma; it's time to fix breakfast."

Back in the kitchen, she can hear her husband's deep commanding voice, "All right boys, it's time to milk the cows. Let's get a move on."

The boys tumble out of their warm bed. They know to do less will incur their father's wrath. Nobody wants to do that. In a matter of minutes, they hurry out of their room, grab their milking pails, and dash away to the barn to begin their morning chores.

Their father is a big man, strong, gruff as a grizzly and as unrelenting as a barbed-wire fence. In reality, his harshness is only a facade. Underneath it all, he is a gentle, kind-hearted man. He had been a strikingly handsome young man, but the ravages of time have taken their toll. Now his appearance is big, strong, and intimidating. He is the type of man whom other men respect and admire. His children feel the need to walk softly in his presence. Nothing, man, woman or beast, intimidates Almeda.

The male members of the family milk the cows, gather the eggs, feed and care for the animals. While Madden and the boys do their chores, the women bake biscuits for breakfast and cookies for the children's lunches. They scramble eggs, fry ham, and make flour gravy. There are also hot-buttered biscuits with honey. Breakfast is ready when the men return from their chores. The adults drink coffee; the children drink fresh milk. Everything, except the coffee, has been produced on their farm.

Almeda insists on saying grace. No one can touch a fork until everybody is ready to eat, and no one can leave the table until everyone is through. We discuss the events of the day and everyone knows what everyone else will be doing. For Almeda, mealtime is more than a time for feeding the body; it is also a time to feed the mind. Conversation and debate is encouraged.

After breakfast, the children must be gotten off to school. Their clothes must be clean, lunches prepared and packed. Almeda makes sure they have their homework with them as they leave.

She then helps Madden prepare for tending the fields. If he needs help, she will be there, ready, willing and able to do whatever is needed. After she has gotten everybody off, her day is just beginning.

The dishes must be washed and the house cleaned. She uses soap she has made from the waste oil from her cooking

Her broom has been made by tying broom weeds to a stout stick.

She then goes to the garden, tills it with a hoe, plants seeds in the warm moist soil, which will in time produce the vegetables for feeding her family. When she harvests the vegetables, she will preserve the extras by canning them in Mason jars. The preserved food will be served in winter, when there is nothing to be harvested from the garden.

Once each week, she washes and irons the clothes. Before she can wash, she must heat the water in a large cast-iron pot. She draws water from the well, gathers wood, builds a fire in the backyard, and then places the pot on the fire. She will dip the hot water from the pot, pour it into a washtub, and blend the hot water with cold water, to attain the proper temperature. The clothes will be scrubbed by using a corrugated metal board. She uses lye soap she has made herself that irritates her hands. After wringing the clothes by hand, she dries them on a smooth wire, which has been drawn between two poles. The sun and wind will do the drying. The dried clothes will be gathered, starched, and ironed, using starch she has made from corn grown in the fields. The irons will be heated on the kitchen stove. After the clothes are ironed, she folds and puts them away, mends what needs mending. Anything too damaged, she cuts into pieces for making quilts. She makes new clothes to replace the ones that been have worn out.

At midday, she prepares dinner for her husband. If she has spare time in the afternoon, she will lower the quilting frame from the ceiling and work at making quilts.

About four o'clock in the afternoon, she starts preparing supper as the children will be returning from school and her husband will be returning from the fields. He will be tired and dirty. He and the children will attend to their own baths, but she must have clean clothes and towels ready.

When the evening meal is through, the dishes will again be cleaned, and the kitchen made ready for cooking tomorrow's breakfast. With the household tasks completed, she will doctor her family's aches and pains. The medicines she uses are mostly of her own making. She uses soap and hot water to cleanse wounds, and then swabs the wounds with kerosene to prevent infection. If she can get aspirin, she will use it for relieving pain. Laxatives are made from a plant that grows wild along the creeks. The medicine is called Black Draught. It tastes terrible. The family calls it Black Death.

Almeda and her husband have had only a limited education. When they can, they help the children with their homework. Then the family sits and talks, plays games such as dominos, checkers, chess, or cards. Sometimes she and her husband tell stories of how it was when they were growing up. The children like to hear the stories their mother tells of coming west in a covered wagon. They never tire of hearing stories of their father's experiences in the war. They also enjoy stories about Grandfather's knowledge of, and in some instances, associations with the outlaw gangs that roamed the west.

After everyone is bedded down, Almeda will blow out the lights and go to the bed she shares with her husband. Th sounds of her sleeping family, the mournful howling of the coyotes, and the call of the night birds lulls her to sleep.

Her life is hard, but she would not trade the life she has for the life of anyone she has ever heard of.

Few statues have been built and few memorials erected to honor the women of the West, but Almeda and thousands of women like her, are truly the people who won the West.

A brief moment in time
William Wayne Dicksion

0-595-34594-8

Printed in the United States
26043LVS00001B/106-138